A MOMENT TO TREASURE

Humming an off-key tune, three slow beats to the measure, Hetty placed her hand stiffly on Jared's shoulder as they prepared to practice the waltz.

"You must relax," he advised, before taking her in a scandalously close embrace. "Just to guide you," he said gruffly, excruciatingly aware of her fragrance, a whisper of lavender.

Humming in deep resonant tones, in perfect pitch, Jared guided her through the steps, their speed increasing as they grew accustomed to the feel of the rhythm of the music. Laughing at the sheer freedom they felt, they moved as one. His voice rising in a closing crescendo, Jared gave Hetty a final twirl. He lost his footing on the grass and fell on his backside, his feet tangled in Hetty's skirts. She landed on top of him, suffering more from a fit of the giggles than any injury.

Her laughter was contagious, and Jared joined in, wrapping his arms around her as she rested her head on his chest, gasping for air. She rolled onto the grass, still laughing, and Jared followed, leaning over her and gazing down at her smiling face.

Her giggles stopped. Jared's smile faded. His eyes sought her lips. Her breathing stilled as she waited for his kiss. . . .

BOOK YOUR PLACE ON OUR WEBSITE AND MAKE THE READING CONNECTION!

We've created a customized website just for our very special readers, where you can get the inside scoop on everything that's going on with Zebra, Pinnacle and Kensington books.

When you come online, you'll have the exciting opportunity to:

- View covers of upcoming books
- Read sample chapters
- Learn about our future publishing schedule (listed by publication month *and author*)
- Find out when your favorite authors will be visiting a city near you
- Search for and order backlist books from our online catalog
- Check out author bios and background information
- Send e-mail to your favorite authors
- Meet the Kensington staff online
- Join us in weekly chats with authors, readers and other guests
- Get writing guidelines
- AND MUCH MORE!

**Visit our website at
http://www.zebrabooks.com**

WORDS OF LOVE

Donna Bell

Zebra Books
Kensington Publishing Corp.
http://www.zebrabooks.com

ZEBRA BOOKS are published by

Kensington Publishing Corp.
850 Third Avenue
New York, NY 10022

First Printing: October, 1999
10 9 8 7 6 5 4 3 2 1

Printed in the United States of America

For the wonderful members of
the Regency Loop, who have helped
me with the research questions and
moral support.
Also for Gayle, who refrains
from calling me the "p" word—
procrastinator!
And for my husband, who has
done so many dishes while I
write.

One

If a star were confin'd into a tomb,
  Her captive flames must needs burn there;
But when the hand that locked her up, gives room,
  She'll shine through all the sphere.
                                    —Henry Vaughan

"Henrietta, my girl, I had no idea you were in London." The starchy dame, dressed from head to toe in black, raised her lorgnette and stared down her long nose at her niece.

Lady Henrietta blanched as she faced her terribly proper aunt, but she did not flinch. Though her inner thoughts might be cursing and moaning, she did not give vent to her frustration. Instead, she smiled and said calmly, "Indeed, Aunt, I have been here some time. Allow me to present my young friend, Miss Margaret Armistead." She turned to the quaking girl by her side with a tight smile, encouraging her to make a slight bow from the carriage.

"Armistead? I know of no Armisteads. Oh yes, there was an Armistead family from someplace up north." The tight-lipped matron studied the girl through her lorgnette. Her aunt was a snob who refused to acknowledge anybody who was not somebody. Accordingly, she demanded, "Are you related to the Yorkshire Armisteads, girl?"

"I-I am not certain, ma'am, though we may be," squeaked Hetty's young charge.

"I daresay there is a connection, Aunt Mary. If you will excuse me, I have a fitting at two o'clock. So good to see you again," lied Hetty, jiggling the reins so her old mare would plod forward, taking them away from her dragon aunt.

When they were alone, she glanced at the girl by her side and smiled.

"Normally, Margaret, a teacher would never encourage a pupil to tell a lie. However, when one is faced with one's most terrifying relative, a tiny untruth might be considered if not precisely moral, then certainly advisable."

"Who was she?" Margaret asked, her eyes still wide.

"That, my dear, was my father's elder sister, Lady Mary Elizabeth Thompson. She never married; couldn't find anyone up to her standards. Rumor has it a Mr. Brown offered for her, but she was unwilling to give up her title," Hetty added. Her ready smile peeked out before she added sternly, "But a lady never gossips, of course, so you will forget my lapse of good manners."

"Of course, Miss Thompson," said the girl, a knowing smile softening her sharp nose and chin.

* * *

When Hetty descended the stairs of her small house on Cavendish Square the next morning, her ancient butler informed her dolefully that two visitors awaited her in the salon.

"It is his grace and Mr. Bigglesby," he said. "His grace indicated the reason for his early visit was momentous."

Drat Aunt Mary anyway! thought Hetty. She should have known her aunt would run straight to Harry! What a way to begin her day!

"Thank you, Sanders. I appreciate your telling me," said Hetty, rolling her eyes. Hetty checked her hair in the hall's oval mirror and smoothed her gown. Taking a deep breath, she entered the salon.

"Good morning, gentlemen. What a delightful surprise!" she said, trying to sound sincere. Not, of course, that she didn't enjoy her brother's company. Harry was normally the best of fellows, until he decided to act the part of family patriarch.

"Good morning, Lady Henrietta—er, I mean, Miss Thompson," said Perry Bigglesby, her brother's friend and Hetty's perpetual suitor. "You're looking very well," he added, bowing from his great height.

"Thank you, Mr. Bigglesby. Is that a new coat? It is quite handsome," she added, smiling at his ready blush.

"Coming it a bit too brown." Her brother gave her cheek a quick buss before saying bluntly, "You went for a drive in the park yesterday, didn't you?"

"Since you are already in possession of that information, Harold, I don't see why you bother asking. Aunt Mary told you, I suppose."

"She wondered about the girl with you."

"You mean my student?" Hetty supplied helpfully, carefully keeping her smile in place. "I *am* a teacher, Harry."

"I remember, sister, much to my annoyance. It was one thing when you wouldn't settle on one of your suitors, but then you started bringing home strays! Amy and I have tried to look the other way, but you promised you would refrain from flaunting your employment in public!"

He paused for breath, a sure sign he was not finished. Hetty said sharply, "Poppycock! Why do you persist in vexing me, Harold? You know very well I have no intention of doing as you say, not on this point. One would think after all these years you would simply accept that fact. Tell him, won't you, Mr. Bigglesby?"

The silent Perry Bigglesby shifted uneasily from one foot to the other. Long acquaintance did not render him comfortable when his oldest friend's sister was being stubborn, something she did regularly, and his friend's jaw was equally set.

Then the glimmer of a smile crossed the sturdy face of the Duke of Bosworth. He could never stay angry long enough to win an argument with his twin. And she was right, as usual.

"Ah," she said, nodding, "you do agree with me. I can see it in your eyes. Then we may be friends again."

Her brother grinned. "I would not put it in those terms, Hetty, but I will quit badgering you for the moment . . . until you do something else outrageous to bring disgrace on the family."

Henrietta's face darkened in warning. "What harm came of showing Hyde Park to young Margaret?" she demanded. "There was no one about, except Aunt Mary!"

"There could be talk, as I have informed you before. Someone seeing you might get the wrong idea. With your coloring and hers being so similar, anyone other than Aunt Mary might have assumed she was your child."

"Harry, Margaret is seventeen. That would mean I was only eleven years old when she was born!"

Not ready to give up his argument, Harry blustered, "I know that, and Aunt Mary does, too, but anyone else? 'Twould be quite a scandal, since you have never married."

Hetty rolled her eyes. "If you intend to belabor that point again, Harold, I swear I will have Sanders throw you out! Besides, people would be much more likely to assume you had merely given over to me the care of one your by-blows," she added outrageously.

The notion of her starchy brother having sired a love child was preposterous, and all knew Hetty's remark was calculated to inflame the duke. Dark brown eyes met golden brown in a battle of wills. The twins, so much alike despite being the opposite sex, tried to glare each other down. It was Harold who yielded first this time, his good nature breaking through with a laugh.

"I can only hope that one day, Hetty, you will come

to your senses and rejoin society. You cannot continue to live your life willy-nilly, any way you please."

"When that day arrives, Harry, I will let you know. Until then, I will live my life as I choose, filling my days with activities that make me feel useful, needed."

"As I have told you before, Amy would love it if you would come live at Bosworth House. And the children . . ."

"Are already spoiled, loved, educated . . . you have no need of me there. Besides," she said, coaxing him with her fond smile, "I do enjoy teaching children, Harold. I feel I was made for it. Surely you wouldn't wish to deprive me of something that brings me joy."

"Humph," he grunted, and Hetty knew she had won another point. She was careful not to gloat, for that would only start the process over again.

"You will join us for Christmas at Bosworth, won't you?"

"Of course I shall! I am so looking forward to it! And I know Daisy is, too," said Hetty, skillfully changing the subject.

"Daisy! How you can call that huge mare of yours Daisy is beyond me! I do wish you would permit me to find you a suitable mount. You really shouldn't . . ." he trailed off, realizing he was treading on thin ice. If there was one thing his stubborn sister would not permit, it was any hint of disapprobation about the beloved old mare their father had given her at the age of eight. And, he admitted privately, Hetty had always been a much better judge of horseflesh than he. If she wanted a new, stylish mount, she was definitely the best person to choose it.

"Come along, Perry, we really should be going. I had no idea of the time," he lied, grinning again.

"Thank you for coming, Mr. Bigglesby. I do hope our little family discussion has not made you too uncomfortable to accompany me to the theatre tonight. Shall I see you this evening at eight?" asked Hetty.

"Quite looking forward to it, my dear," said her brother's friend.

Hetty cringed inside at his eager smile. It had been some time since Bigglesby had proposed marriage to her. She supposed he had decided tonight, in his box at the theatre, would be yet another opportunity.

Turning back to her brother, she grinned and said, "Please come again, Harry. I do so enjoy our little debates."

"As do I, *little* sister. As do I."

The door closed behind her erstwhile suitor and her very proper brother before she could retort that the three minutes that separated them by birth were not sufficient to make her a little sister, not to mention the fact that she towered above her diminutive brother.

Glancing in the gilded mirror by the door, Hetty smoothed her brown hair and took a deep breath before joining her first pupil of the day in the small study. After the proper exchange of greetings and comments on the weather, Hetty handed the girl a slate that contained several problems in addition.

While Margaret worked, Hetty completed the menu for dinner.

"Miss Thompson, can you check these before I go on? I don't think I'm doing them right," the girl said, frowning at the slate. Such simple arithmetic should have been too easy for a girl of her age, but Margaret had great difficulty with numbers. She read beautifully, but mathematics was her nemesis.

Hetty quickly added the long columns of figures. "You have done very well, Margaret. I find only one mistake. It is in the third problem. See if you can discover it while I ring for tea."

When Hetty returned, the girl's plain face was wreathed in smiles.

"I forgot to add the last one in the ten column, didn't I?"

"That's right. Now we are ready for your tea lesson. Your father told me he was much impressed the last time you poured out for him."

"Did he really?" asked the girl eagerly.

"Yes, he said you acted like a real lady. High praise, indeed," said Hetty, watching intently as her pupil rose and moved to the sofa, waiting politely for Hetty to be seated before taking her own place and smoothing her short gown carefully.

"Won't you pour, Miss Armistead?"

"I would be delighted," said Margaret, taking a deep breath before picking up the delicate china teapot.

"Very nicely done," said Hetty, smiling at the shy girl.

"Thank you, Miss Thompson."

"Hasn't the weather been lovely?" Hetty remarked, after a moment of silence that threatened to be awkward.

"Yes, quite." The girl appeared to be working out some problem, for she was frowning ferociously.

Gently, Hetty asked, "Was there something you

wished to talk about, Margaret? We can forget about practicing polite conversation if there is."

"No—yes—I mean, you will think I am terribly curious, Miss Thompson, but I have been wondering ever since we met your aunt in the park yesterday . . ."

"Yes? You may feel free to speak," said Hetty.

"You said she was Lady Thompson, but my father says I should have called her Lady Bosworth."

"No, Lady Mary Thompson. She was the daughter of the duke, not the wife," explained Hetty. "She uses the family surname, not the name of the dukedom."

"I see. But doesn't that make *you* the daughter of a duke?" asked the gal in awe-stricken tones.

Privately, Hetty thought the girl was too clever for her own good—or at least for Hetty's good. She gave a tight smile and said, "That is not something I want the world to know, Margaret. I'm sure you can understand."

"But I shouldn't be calling you Miss Thompson, Miss Thompson, I should be calling you Lady Something."

"Margaret, allow me to tell you a secret. You must promise me this will go no further. You especially shouldn't tell your father."

The wide-eyed girl nodded.

"If I wanted to go by Lady Henrietta, I could. But the truth of the matter is I much prefer being plain Miss Thompson, teacher to Miss Margaret Armistead. Lady Henrietta doesn't exist anymore, except, of course, when I visit my family. Even then, I am just plain Hetty. So you see, I don't want you to call me Lady Henrietta. Miss Thompson suits me fine. What's more, I can't abide my full name, Henrietta," confided Hetty.

"If you say so, Miss Thompson," said Margaret, happily continuing her lesson in the social graces.

According to the girl's father, this was the most important part of Margaret's education. He was a banker in the City, a position that placed him far below Lady Henrietta Thompson, the daughter of the duke of Bosworth, but he wanted the very best for his motherless child. Had he known Hetty's true identity, he would have been too intimidated by her rank to hire her as his daughter's tutor.

He didn't know, of course. Hetty had taken the small house on Cavendish Street, assumed the name of Henrietta Thompson, and advertised her "Tutorial Services in the Social Graces." At first, there had been few takers. In the past three years, she had worked with one or two children at a time. Then Mr. Armistead had arrived on her doorstep.

The late Mrs. Armistead, he had informed Hetty proudly when trying to persuade her to be Margaret's full-time tutor, was the daughter of a baronet. When the time came, he wanted Margaret to be able to look higher than a cit for her own husband.

Margaret's doting father, though he was only ten years Hetty's senior, reminded Hetty of her own father, who had loved his only daughter dearly. Unfortunately, the late Duke of Bosworth had been terrified his daughter would accept an offer from a fortune hunter and had spent the last years of his life warning her of dire consequences if she didn't guard her heart. He had meant well, Hetty admitted to herself, but the result had been an unhappy one.

Meeting Margaret, Hetty had been taken back to her own days at finishing school, which had rendered an already shy girl, a virtual recluse. She'd had nothing in common with the other girls. Her great loves had been horses, riding, and the country. She had cared nothing for a Season in London, and it had proven a total disaster. Had it not been for Perry Bigglesby, whom she regarded more as a brother than a beau, her four Seasons before her father died would have been unbearable.

Tonight, when Perry took her to the theatre, she would do her best to dissuade him from proposing. He was such a dear friend.

The morning drew to a close, and Hetty waved good-bye to her first pupil. At one o'clock, another pupil, this one requiring only lessons in French and the social graces, would appear on her doorstep. When his lessons were over, Hetty would take the carriage out and drive to the country. There, dressed in a simple gown and cloak, she could enjoy a solitary stroll without the danger of offending either Society or her straight-laced brother.

Hetty waved good-bye to her afternoon pupil with a sigh. The boy was growing like a weed, his voice squeaking every other word. Soon Cecil would have no need of her. By the spring term, he would be ready for school.

The sun was going down, and Hetty took the tinderbox and lighted the candles in the wall sconces and in the candelabra. Then she crossed to the windows. The lamplighter was busy putting his torch to the lamps that lined the street, giving the avenue a soft glow. This was perhaps her favorite time of year. The little Season was almost over, and London was practically empty of Society. She could come and go as she pleased.

At eight and twenty, Hetty felt she had earned the right to her privacy, but in London, prying eyes and tattling mouths were everywhere. How they could find entertainment in the activities of an aging spinster was beyond her, but they never ceased to interest themselves in the sister of a duke.

She had been teaching for the past three years, an employment which she considered a service to the needy. The parents of her students were usually quite wealthy, and they spared no expense trying to turn their offspring into gentlewomen and gentlemen. Their births rendered them unacceptable to the *ton,* of course, but Hetty found them, for the most part, quite admirable. Her children were nothing like the spoiled daughters of the *ton* who had studied at Miss Brown's Seminary for Young Ladies. Hetty's students actually wanted to learn to perfect their manners and improve their speech.

Her occupation, should the *ton* learn of it, would put her beyond the pale. A few people knew, of course, but by agreement with her brother, she didn't bruit it about. There were her twin nieces to consider. They were only seven, but time passed so quickly.

"A person to see you, Miss Thompson," announced

Sanders, his voice strong despite the manner in which his fragile old body swayed to and fro in the doorway.

"Show him in," said Hetty.

Sanders sometimes forgot faces, but the small, ferret-like man who entered was indeed a stranger to her. Sanders hovered by the door, his presence comforting her.

She suddenly wished she had more servants. There was only one able-bodied male in the household who might be able to protect its mistress. Ned worked in the garden and would come running with his hoe if he heard her scream.

But the weasely man bowed deferentially and offered her his card, saying, "I apologize for not giving this to your man there, madam, but my request requires the utmost discretion, and if you should turn down my offer, I didn't want to give away too much information."

Glancing at the card, Hetty said, "I understand, Mr. Norton. Won't you be seated?"

He took the least comfortable chair, a sure sign he knew his place. Glancing toward the doorway furtively, he cleared his throat. Hetty motioned Sanders away, and the door closed softly. She knew he would stand beside the door, on guard lest she should need him.

"What may I do for you, Mr. Norton?"

"I was given your name, Miss Thompson, as a tutor of the social graces. A lady, if you please, who can take the most disgraceful scamp and turn him into a real gentleman."

"I'm not certain what you have heard, or from

whom, Mr. Norton, but I do tutor children in the rudimentaries of academics, in elocution, and in the social niceties. Do you have a child in need of my services?"

"Not me, ma'am, not exactly. My employer, that is, the estate of my late employer, is in need of your services. We have traced the next heir to the colonies—the United States, that is—and before he can take his place in Society, we feel certain he will be in need of some instruction."

"I see. How old is the boy?"

"I'm not sure, but he can't be more than fifteen or sixteen. I only discovered his existence when I was going through my client's papers. He is the second son of the late marquess's brother. I believe the first child perished making the journey to America. Because of the difficulty in recent years, I was unable to discover his whereabouts until recently."

"I see. I'm afraid my schedule is a bit full at the moment, Mr. Norton. I might be able to work with him for an hour in the late afternoon . . ."

"I don't think you understand, Miss Thompson. I need someone to work with his lordship around the clock. We have no idea how deficient he may be in certain areas."

His lordship, thought Hetty. All her other students were the children of working people—solicitors, manufacturers, and such. She had never had to deal with people of her own class.

"Surely a tutor, perhaps a retired headmaster, would be a better choice."

"We assume the boy has been schooled in the traditional manner, so he shouldn't need instruction in the classics or the sciences. What we want is to make certain he understands his duty. One day, he will take up the reins as master of a large estate. It is hoped he will take his place as a welcome member of Society, as well as a member of Parliament. We may even send him to university after some time, but first the boy must learn what it means to be a peer, something you are eminently qualified to teach the lad."

"But my schedule . . ."

"I am authorized to pay any amount, Miss Thompson, although I know money is not of paramount importance to someone in your position," he said, his beady eyes taking in the simple but elegant furnishings.

Hetty shifted uncomfortably on her chair. What, exactly, was this man about? Did he know her true identity? Was he trying to blackmail her or her family? Well, he would find himself out of luck if that were the case. She would simply shut up the house and return to Bosworth. Her brother would be ecstatic.

"Mr. Norton, I appreciate your predicament, but I think you should find someone else," she said slowly, studying his reaction.

"No one would be as suitable as you, Miss Thompson. Only consider the plight of this poor young man. He may be as well-educated as any of our lads, but he has been reared in the wilderness. His mother was a nobody, his father only a second son. The late marquess had three boys, but each died in childhood. His brother had no idea his own son would inherit the title and vast holdings. He could not possibly have prepared the boy for this heavy burden. No matter how bright the lad is, he will not fit in. His speech alone will set him apart. And can you imagine how he will be treated by the other students at Oxford?"

Hetty nibbled on her lower lip, her brow furrowed. In the face of this extraordinary need, how could she refuse? The boy would be lost at Oxford. Youth was never kind to anyone who was different. Her own years at Miss Brown's Seminary for Young Ladies had been fraught with misery. She had never fit in with the empty-headed girls interested only in dancing and music.

But Mr. Norton was waiting, watching. Reaching a decision, Hetty asked, "When would I need to begin?"

"Not until I fetch him back to England. Two, perhaps three months, at least."

Hetty knew Margaret would be going to visit an aunt in Bath for the spring and would no longer need her services. Cecil Deavers would be attending public school during the next term. Really, this offer might be the answer to a prayer.

Smiling, she said, "Very well, Mr. Norton, I will tutor your charge. Only let me know when you have returned."

"Thank you, Miss Thompson, thank you so very much. This is quite a weight off my mind. I can make my journey to America with a lighter heart knowing my charge will be well looked after on our return. As to the particulars, I know you will appreciate that we act in the utmost secrecy. No one must know of our endeavor until we are ready to spring the new marquess on the world."

"I understand, Mr. Norton. Only tell me where the

estate is, and I will be in residence when you return with the boy."

"I'm afraid I haven't made myself clear, Miss Thompson. I think it would be better if the child came here to London."

"Here?"

"Yes. He has a town house of his own, but it has been shut up for some years, so I have taken the liberty of securing a small but comfortable house on South Audley."

"But surely his estate in the country would be the best setting," said Hetty.

"I'm afraid not. There are certain family members who reside at his country seat who would be only too happy to spread gossip about the boy. And if I were to open his town house in London . . . well, you understand. I wouldn't wish to expose him to the meddlesome society of his peers before he is ready. And even if you and I were to keep our own counsel, you know how servants talk. The anonymity of this new house is much wiser, don't you agree?"

He didn't pause long enough for her to comment, but continued, "I will hire a suitable staff, of course. You may wish to bring your maid, but all the rest will be taken care of, including a housekeeper. You will not have to bother yourself with the running of the house. You may concentrate on your pupil's progress completely." He sat back with a satisfied sigh.

Hetty frowned. She loved her snug little house on Cavendish Street. How could she leave it and her servants? They were like family. Still, there were too many people who knew the true identity of the mistress of this house. Though she no longer aspired to move in the high circles her birth would allow, she did not wish to be the center of a scandal. Living in this house with a young man, though he was hardly more than a child, would spell disaster for everyone concerned. It would be best, she reluctantly admitted, if the deed was carried out in secret.

Hetty returned her attention to the man before her, who seemed intent on outlining every servant he would hire and what their numerous duties would be. Hetty, who cared next to nothing for such matters, held up her hand for silence.

"As for moving to South Audley, Mr. Norton, I am willing to do so, but you must allow me to take two of my servants with me. My butler and personal maid are completely reliable. I will not consider such a move without them. Oh, and you will need to hire suitable quarters for my horse and groom. I have no desire to be hiring a hack every time I wish to go for a ride."

"Of course, of course, anything you wish, Miss Thompson," said the solicitor, rising. "Then we are agreed. I can't tell you how relieved I am that I can leave my charge in your capable hands. Thank you, Miss Thompson, and good day. I will see you after Christmas, hopefully by the end of January. Should you incur any expenses on behalf of my client, just forward the bills to my office. My man will be in touch with the particulars for your move. And thank you again."

"You're welcome, Mr. Norton. I feel certain your

young charge and I will rub along quite well. I am looking forward to learning about his life in America."

"Such an uncivilized place," murmured Mr. Norton, bowing slightly as he backed toward the door. "Good day."

Hetty settled back against the smooth sofa with a sigh. She prayed she had done the right thing. A boy of fifteen or sixteen was almost not a boy. She smiled.

What on earth was she worrying about? It was not as if he would view her as anything other than a too strict, old-fashioned teacher. If she were beautiful, she might have to worry he would form some improper attachment to her, but Hetty had never been much bothered by the attentions of a man, much less a boy.

Despite her quiet demeanor, she had received numerous offers during her Seasons in London. The daughter of a duke who was possessed not only of an excellent dowry but also of a tidy independence could expect to be courted by certain members of the *ton*. But she had never been able to overcome the lowering suspicion none of her beaux wanted her for the beauty of herself—except Perry, of course, and she did not love him.

Still, she concluded, returning to her self-contemplation, she was comforted by the knowledge that, had she chosen to do so, she could have been wed any number of times, if only the right man had come along.

"Good evening, Mr. Bigglesby. You are looking very dapper tonight. Another new coat? You are becoming quite the fashion plate," Hetty teased.

He smiled and nodded. "I was hoping you would notice, Miss Thompson."

"Come in, do, and have a seat. I thought we could have dinner in here at the backgammon table. I had Sanders set it for us. It is so much more cozy than the dining room, don't you think?"

The obliging Mr. Bigglesby inspected the table near the fire, laid with the best plate, and smiled again, nodding several times.

"I'm so glad you approve. It may seem forward of me, but we are such old friends I knew no one would look askance at this little *dîner à deux.*"

Mr. Bigglesby was not the slow-top some people took him for, despite his plodding speech. He turned from the table and studied her for a moment before that rare grin that lighted his pale-blue eyes appeared. Hetty said nothing, only nodded and smiled in return.

She indicated the place beside her on the sofa, saying, "Now we may be comfortable together."

"Very well, my dear," said Perry, joining her.

"I was wondering if you are really set on going to the theater tonight, Perry," she said, her expression earnest.

Her usage of his given name, so seldom heard since they had reached maturity, startled him.

"If you want to see—what is it that is playing?— then of course we shall go," she added.

"No, no, I only thought you wanted to, Miss Hetty."

"Oh, good. You see . . ."

Sanders entered, followed by the maid, who carried an immense tray. Efficiently, they set the tray on the sideboard and stood at attention while Mr. Bigglesby escorted Hetty to the table.

When they had been served the first course and the servants had retired, Hetty asked, "How long have we known each other?"

"You and Harry were ten when he brought me home from Eton for the holidays. That's eighteen years ago."

"Exactly. And of that eighteen years, how many have you spent professing to love me?"

He shifted uncomfortably in his chair and appeared unable or unwilling to reply. Hetty waited patiently, but she refused to supply the answer, though she knew it as well as he.

Mr. Bigglesby cleared his throat and ran a hand through his crop of thinning red curls. Finally, taking a deep breath as if for strength, he replied, "For eighteen years."

"Perry—and I use your given name because that is what close friends do—you must realize after eighteen years my answer is not going to change. Would you have me send you away, a man whom I consider my best friend, because you cannot let go of this childhood infatuation?"

"But, Miss . . ."

"Hetty," she said firmly and with great kindness. "You must call me Hetty if I am to remain your friend."

"Very well, Hetty, but you know I am sincere. What would you have me do? Marry elsewhere when my heart is pledged to you?"

"Fiddlesticks!"

"Hetty!"

"Fiddlesticks, I say! Perry, if you truly loved me, you would have been pining away all these years. You would have . . . oh, I don't know, thrown yourself in front of a stampeding carriage."

"Now who is being facetious?" asked Perry Bigglesby, that grin breaking forth once more. "So what are you saying, Hetty? You want me to leave you alone?"

"Not alone, Perry."

"You know what I mean. I am to cease badgering you about marrying me?"

"Yes, old friend, but that is not all. I want you to go out and find you someone you can truly love, body and soul, and who will love you back the same way."

"You know, Hetty, I do believe you are romantical. I never guessed. Then again, you were never so with me," said Mr. Bigglesby, turning his thoughts inward.

Hetty reached across the small table and patted his beefy hand.

"We are still friends, aren't we?"

For just a moment when he looked up at her, she could see in his unshuttered eyes a depth of feeling she had never guessed. It vanished quickly, and he grasped her hand, nodding.

"The very best," he said.

They ate in silence for a few minutes, each lost in thought.

Then Perry cocked his head to one side, his eyes began to dance, and he said, "You know, Hetty, I am not very good at these social gatherings where one must go to meet young ladies. I hope you are prepared to join me during the coming Season and help me find a suitable wife."

Hetty's mouth worked furiously for a moment. Then she laughed. "You trickster! I was going to say Harry put you up to this. Then I remembered I have no one to thank but myself!"

"So you'll help?"

"Yes, Perry, I'll help. But do not tax me on the subject, else I am likely to choose a harridan for you instead of the sweet, malleable bride you deserve!"

It was late before Perry Bigglesby left her. They had enjoyed a wonderful evening, reminiscing about holidays when the three of them had terrorized the neighborhood with their childish escapades.

"Will you be needing anything else, miss?" asked Molly.

Hetty shook her head, but the maid remained next to the door. Finally, Hetty asked, "Was there something else you needed, Molly?"

"I just wanted to make sure you were all right, miss," said the maid, curtsying.

Hetty smiled and replied gently, "Yes, Molly, I am fine. And Mr. Bigglesby is fine, too. We are still friends."

Molly, who had been with Hetty since her first Season in London, smiled. "I'm that glad, I am, miss. Good night."

"Good night, Molly," said Hetty.

She climbed into bed, snuggling under the counterpane and hugging the evening's memories to herself.

It was good to have her old friend back. There would no longer be that barrier between them, no more holding herself aloof to guard against hurting him.

Hetty stared at the top of the bed's canopy, a confection of a rare yellow velvet and tulle. On the pillow beside her slept her small foxhound, snoring softly. Unaccountably, Hetty's spirits began to sink, though she tried to rally by swathing herself in more childhood recollections.

Longings, romantical longings . . . could she ever escape from them? The answer drove her out of the comfortable bed to the chair by the fire. Passing the full-length cheval glass, she paused, leaning toward it, studying her figure in the firelight.

Still slender, she decided, *though the dressmaker probably despairs from time to time in fitting gowns over my generous bosom.*

Hetty turned sideways.

Still, it is not huge or out of proportion to the rest of me, she comforted herself. Stepping closer, she analyzed her face, confessing with ruthless honesty that the firelight softened the years.

Not a beautiful face, she told herself as always, *but not ugly, either. If only the fashion were for downy waves instead of ringlets, something I will never achieve. . . . My nose is a bit too long, but I'm hardly an antidote. Now, that mouth is perhaps a trifle wide, but that young man—what was his name?—anyway, he said he loved women with wide, willing mouths.*

Hetty smiled at her reflection, recalling her brother's reaction when she had asked him what the gentleman meant by that. He hadn't responded, but his high color

had challenged her to ever mention it again. That had
been eight years ago, in her second Season.

Hetty frowned and moved to the chair, lighting a
candle and picking up a novel from the table at her
elbow. If there was one thing she was not ready to
admit, it was that she still longed for a man, a lover,
to come and sweep her off her feet.

She opened to the first page and began to read.

Two

. . . And then the whining schoolboy, with his satchel
And shining morning face, creeping like snail
Unwillingly to school. . . .

—Shakespeare

"Put him back in the cell," growled the old judge, his face red with anger. "And you can throw away the key for all I care," he grumbled.

Jared grinned as the constable led him away again. There had been little enough to smile about in the past few months. He would take his humor, be it ever so slight, wherever he might. The corrupt old judge was frustrated. *Better he than I,* thought Jared.

The grin faded when he reentered the fetid jail. He would never grow accustomed to the odor of unwashed bodies and excrement. He could close his eyes and dream he was under a blue sky, his face warmed by bright sunshine, but the stench always dragged him back to reality, to the prison cell where he had dwelled for almost two months while they debated every minute aspect of each charge.

He was getting discouraged, something he rarely allowed to happen. He had lived by his wits for too many years to fall into that trap. There was always a way out, always another turn of a card. This last effort by Crenshaw had been a near thing. If Angel had not come forward to swear he had spent the night in her bed. . . .

Jared smiled again. It had almost been worth the ordeal of this entire sham of a trial to watch the lecherous judge and prosecutor drool over Angel as she plied her lacy handkerchief, covering her dry eyes and pretending to weep. And then there was the satisfaction of knowing Angel's lie had thwarted Crenshaw's vengefulness again.

"Mr. Winter?"

"Yes," he said cautiously, eyeing the tall, burly man in rough homespun. He swung his legs over the side of the cot and sat up.

"My name's Turner. The judge said I was to talk to you. I need some information." The visitor studied Jared, a frown furrowing his beefy brow.

Jared waited, wondering why the hair on the back of his neck was standing on end. He tried to shake free from his unease and smiled at the man.

"How much do you weigh?" asked the mountain.

"Why?"

"I take pride in my work, Mr. Winter. I want everything to finish up nice and tidy."

"And what work is that?"

"I'm the hangman. Not many people like to talk to me about the subject, but I do want everything nice and neat. I have to know how much you weigh, or all sorts of bad things might happen. The rope might break . . ."

"Not an unpleasant prospect, from my point of view," said Jared, his throat dry with fear.

"Heh, heh, guess ye're right there, Mr. Winter. But it only makes it last longer. So you see, it's in yer best interest to tell me how much you weigh, Mr. Winter."

"Mr. Jared Winter?" called another voice from the open doorway.

"What now?" muttered Jared. "Who wants to know?" he said, realizing suddenly he didn't care who it was as long as someone interrupted this grotesque interview.

The fastidious newcomer lowered the handkerchief that covered his nose and mouth. Tucking it into a pocket, he moved forward. Jared hesitated before shaking the man's proffered hand.

"My name is Norton, Tobias Norton. I have some information I think will be of great interest to you."

"Come in, Mr. Norton. Mr. Turner here, our local purveyor of justice, was just leaving," said Jared. In answer to Norton's puzzled mien, he added coldly, "The hangman."

"But I . . ." began Turner.

"Get along with you, my good man," said Norton, ushering the surprised executioner out of the cell. "What I have to discuss with my client is confidential. What's more, when I am finished here, I daresay your services will no longer be needed."

Jared breathed a sigh of relief when the door had closed on Mr. Turner, and he thanked his newest visitor.

"Now, what can I do for you, Mr. Norton? Make yourself at home. Just be careful when you sit in that chair. It's not very sturdy—or very clean, for that matter. I don't get many visitors. I don't rightly count the hangman, but most of my other acquaintances have forgotten about me being in here, it's been so long. Either that, or they just don't care. So have a seat and tell me what brings you to my humble abode."

"Thank you, I will. If you'll excuse me, I need to find the right paper." His visitor sifted through a satchel filled with official-looking documents. Instead of a paper, he pulled out a heavy Bible and handed it to Jared. "First of all, I secured this from a wall safe in your house here in New Orleans. The safe was already open," he added apologetically.

A flash of anger tightened Jared's jaw as he set the book aside. "Nice to know my friends are looking after my interests. But why did you bring me this? I'm not much on praying, though maybe I should try it. Nothing else has worked."

Norton retrieved the book and opened it. "William Harold Winter wed Emily Anne O'Banyon, seventeenth day of July, the year of our Lord, 1784, St. Bernard's Church, Plymouth, England. It is signed by the rector. I verified this at St. Bernard's myself."

"You needn't bother reading my own family history to me, Mr. Norton," said Jared dryly, but the irritating little man raised one hand for silence and continued.

"There is also mention of the birth of a son." Norton looked up, saying, "You, I suppose. Later, there is another child, your younger brother, I believe. May I suggest both of you . . ."

"Never mind about Willie. What is it you want?"

"Hm, let me see. Yes, yes, here it is." Reaching into the leather satchel once more, Norton produced a piece of paper and handed it to Jared. "Do you recognize the names on this paper?"

"Of course I do. These must be my parents' marriage lines. What are you doing with them?"

"Well you may ask," said the solicitor, beaming. "Just for the record, when and where were you born?"

"Why?" asked Jared, his face growing hard. When the solicitor didn't answer, he said curtly, "I was born in England, someplace along the coast, in April of 1785. Two days later, my parents and I sailed for America."

"Excellent, excellent. That concurs with the information I have. Here is the list of passengers from the ship's captain—not that you would remember the crossing, of course. There are your parents' names, and yours, too," said Norton, pointing to the paper. "In the captain's log, there is mention of the death of one infant. When I first read this list, I noticed there were no other babies on board, at least not when they set sail. I assumed, of course, that the deceased infant was you. Obviously, I was in error."

"What is this all about?" demanded Jared, his thin store of patience disintegrating.

"Your father's brother, the Marquess Winter, died three years ago. His issuance—children, that is—died in childhood. He had several nephews, but according to the patent on the title and entail, the holdings revert to his brother. That would be your father."

"My father died in 1803."

"Exactly. At the time, we were notified of his death by a solicitor here in New Orleans, the same one who helped me locate you. Since your father is deceased, as his heir, you stand to inherit the title and the estates that go along with it."

"And the debts, too, no doubt. Thank you, but no thanks, Mr. Norton. I have enough trouble of my own without inheriting more."

"Trouble? Why, this is not trouble, young man. This is a windfall! Do you have any idea how much money and land we are talking about, not to mention the prestige of the title? Why, it is one of the oldest in all of England!"

"Look, I'm certain by English standards this is quite an honor, but I'm not English. I'm an American. I prefer to earn my money."

The solicitor's skeptical gaze traveled slowly around the dimly lighted cell.

Jared grimaced and conceded, "All right, all right, so I've had a few setbacks. But I'll come about. The judge is on the verge of releasing me. He knows he can't make any of the charges stick."

"Ergo, the visit from the hangman," said Norton, not daring to meet Jared's gaze. But he continued without shrinking, "I have read the charges against you. They seem to be rather trivial. I was amazed to learn you had been incarcerated for two months. There was one point I wasn't quite clear on, being English and not American. I was puzzled about the charge which asserted you stole some slaves . . ."

"I didn't steal anything. They weren't slaves. They were freemen, friends of mine. In a manner of speaking, I was renting them out to . . . well, they owed me some money and agreed I might sell them in order to pay their debt," said Jared defensively.

"I assume the buyers were unaware of the transitory nature of their purchase," commented Norton.

Jared laughed. "They seemed to take it in good part after I offered to return their money, but . . ."

"Then there was the matter of a card game?"

Jared winced. He looked up at the solicitor and grinned. "Lady Luck has not been in my pocket lately."

Norton nodded solemnly. "I think I should tell you, I was in the courtroom this afternoon, my lord."

"Don't call me that!"

"And I spoke to the magistrate—"

"The judge."

"Very well then, the judge. I fear he has been presented with new evidence—something about a deck of cards."

"How the devil?" Jared muttered.

"I had a very interesting conversation with the judge. It seems he might be willing to lose this last bit of evidence if you could be persuaded to leave New Orleans in the next few days and not return."

Jared laughed. "I'll just wager he did. Wants me to go away and leave his only daughter alone. He wants her to marry a piece of property." Jared stood up and stretched, dwarfing the small cell. "I doesn't really matter. I was only interested in her to aggravate him, which pleased Miranda, too."

"Nevertheless, if you will leave New Orleans for good, he has agreed to release you."

"That's blackmail." Jared strode the short length of the cell. "You lawyers are all like! You can go to the devil, Norton. I'm not going back to England with you. If you want to help me get out of this mess, I'll be grateful, but I'm not going back to a country where families turn their backs on newborn babies."

Norton watched the younger man with great interest. When his agent had contacted him to confirm the existence of an heir to the marquessate, he hadn't written with specifics. Norton had concluded that the deceased baby mentioned on the ship's passenger list was Winter, just as he had told Miss Thompson. Few infants could survive such a journey, especially when the parents had been unable to afford the luxury of a private cabin. So Norton had assumed the new marquess would be the later child whose existence he had discovered when going through the old marquess's papers.

Norton frowned. Miss Thompson would be surprised to discover her pupil was probably older than she was. Still, this man, though he was two and thirty, would need her help just as much as a youngster. He was quite rough around the edges. Norton sighed. A younger man would have been more malleable.

"If you refuse, you will probably be hanged."

Jared muttered a foul curse before calling, "Jailer!"

"Very well then. What of your brother?" the solicitor asked.

"Brother? Why do you care about my brother?"

"If you refuse the title, it will go to him, regardless if you live or die. So where is he?"

Jared sank down on the bed again. It had been almost fifteen years, and he still found it difficult to speak about his younger brother. At length, he said quietly, "Willie was killed along with my father and mother. Marauders preying on the settlers northwest of New Orleans."

"I see," said Norton, his immediate concern about the inheritance. Looking up, he was moved by the raw pain in his client's eyes. Belatedly, he stammered, "I am sorry, my . . ."

The door opened, and the jailer, pocketing his bribe money, said, "Another visitor for you, Winter."

"Jared!" wailed the teary-eyed vision in white gossamer. She sailed past the jailer, bent over Jared, and clasped him to her generously exposed bosom.

"Angel, Angel, you shouldn't have come. This is no place for you." Jared struggled to detach himself from the clinging female who threatened to suffocate him.

Daintily, she dabbed at her tears and stood up, regarding Norton with open curiosity. "Am I interrupting?"

"Angel Grant, Tobias Norton."

"How do you do, sir? Are you an old friend of Jared's? Please say you are here to help him!"

"No, we have only just met," said Norton, looking alarmed when she heaved a sigh and sank down on the cot. Hastily, he added, "That is, yes, I am here to help, but I have not known Mr. Winter for long, Mrs. Grant," he said, deciding it would be best to err on the side of politeness and employ the title, considering her age. She was not as young as he had at first believed, nor was she likely to be a miss by any stretch of the imagination.

"How like you, Jared, making friends even in this dismal place." She sniffed into her handkerchief again and moaned, "Oh, to find you here, hours from the hangman's noose. I think I shall faint!"

"Cut line, Angel. We both know you hadn't even thought about me until yesterday. By the way, thank you for your testimony."

"It was the least I could do," she said.

"I agree, considering you've been helping yourself to everything I own since I was arrested."

"Why, Jared, darling, how can you be so cruel? I have been absolutely beside myself with grief over your plight."

"Is that why you went through my wall safe?" he demanded before turning to Norton for confirmation. "It was completely empty except for that Bible, wasn't it?"

"Indeed, my lord," said the solicitor.

"I told you not to call me that!" exclaimed Jared.

"My lord? My lord?" said Angel, her protestation instantly silenced as a look of cunning slid across her features before she quickly masked her interest. "Why, I don't know anything about that safe, Jared. You must believe me. It was those nasty officers who arrested you! They took practically everything away, sold most of it . . ."

A heavy knocking interrupted her tale.

The hangman's face appeared in the cell window. "Please, Mr. Winter! I've got to know how much you weigh! I just can't allow you to ruin my reputation! I just talked to th' judge again, an' he says it's urgent!"

Jared Winter had always prided himself on his perspicacity. He fancied he knew when to throw in his hand. Looking past Angel's head, he met Norton's gaze with one of resignation.

"When do we set sail?"

"I do apologize, my lord," whispered the green-faced solicitor for the hundredth time. "I was so hoping I would be better on the way home."

Jared hid his aggravation at Norton's use of the title. The man was too seasick to berate. He placed the clean bucket closer to the berth and dipped a cloth into the basin of cool water.

After bathing the older man's brow, he said quietly, "Just get some sleep, if you can, Norton. You'll feel better in a day or two."

"I pray you are right," came the weak reply.

Jared took a seat in the far corner by the curtained porthole. Picking up a book, he held it to the dim light and read. From time to time, he rose and bathed the solicitor's warm face, but he never left the cabin.

For Jared, the days on board the ship were a time of healing. The air was so crisp and clean, he thought his lungs would burst from pleasure. When he turned his face to the sun, it was brighter than he remembered, and the rain touching his face purged his pallor and his spirit, polishing away the filth and fear of prison.

At night, when Norton was sleeping soundly, Jared

made his way to the deck, found a quiet corner, and gazed at the stars. Though he wouldn't have admitted it to Norton, his imprisonment had been a near thing— not just the threat of death, but the threat to his sanity. He wasn't certain he would have lasted another day. Always a restless spirit, Jared knew if they had not hanged him, he would have found some other way to escape, either physically or mentally.

"Excuse me, Mr. Winter. I don't wish to appear forward, but my husband is playing cards with a few of the passengers, and I seem to have lost my way. Could you direct me to my cabin?"

The night hid Jared's dancing eyes, and he bowed solemnly to the captain's wife, who knew the ship better than he did. But he knew how to play the game, and she had been sending him very definite signals since they had set sail more than a week ago. She was an attractive woman, a little too thin for his liking, but with a feline quality that made promises with every supple movement.

"It would be my pleasure, Mrs. Fox. Right this way," said Jared, presenting his arm.

Mrs. Fox clasped his elbow tightly, pressing her breast against his arm. "It is such a beautiful night, but it is rather chilly, don't you think, Mr. Winter?"

Jared grinned. What else would it be in early January? Still, he said gallantly, "Let me put my coat around your shoulders, Mrs. Fox. I wouldn't want you to catch cold."

She trilled happily and shrugged into his coat before taking his arm possessively again. "My name is Priscilla, Mr. Winter," she said, smiling up at him.

"A lovely name," came his noncommittal reply.

"You're from New Orleans, aren't you?" she asked.

"Yes."

"Were you born there?"

"Actually, I was born in England, but I have lived in the United States all my life."

"In the South, I'll be bound," she purred. "Southern gentlemen are so . . . intriguing."

"Really? Now I have always thought that about Southern women. Intriguingly beautiful, that is," he whispered.

With a pout, she replied, "But I'm from Pennsylvania, Mr. Winter."

"Why, you surprise me, Mrs. Fox. I could have sworn you were a gently reared Southern lady."

She snuggled closer.

"I believe this is your cabin." Jared stopped and drew his coat away from her shoulders.

"Would you care to come in, Mr. Winter? My husband has a bottle of very fine port, and I'm certain he would want me to thank you for your assistance."

Since this last was said while she leaned against his chest, Jared could hardly mistake her message. It had been a long time.

He sighed, smiling as he set her away from him. "I really should be going, ma'am. I think I'll sit in on a hand or two with the captain—your husband. If you'll excuse me?"

She watched his retreat with a pout on her face. Then, ever hopeful, she called, "Another time, perhaps, Mr. Winter."

With a backward wave of his hand, Jared made his

escape. Married women were forbidden fruit to him. He had been tempted from time to time, but he had never taken one to his bed. There had been a number of opportunities, but Jared drew the line at that point. Now, a widow . . . ah, that was another matter, he thought as he whistled his way toward the card game. A shame there weren't any widows on board.

For the duration of the sail, Jared managed to keep the captain's wife at arm's length. It had, at times, been an exercise in monumental self-control. Finally, however, they were closing in on their destination. He was looking forward to saying good-bye to the seductive Mrs. Fox.

Standing at the rail, Jared was joined by the solicitor. "You're looking much better, Norton," he said.

"It's the sight of land, my lord, especially when it is home and I know I don't have to board another boat in a few days." Norton smiled for the first time in four weeks.

"Odd, but it doesn't strike me the same way." Jared had come to ignore the frequent "my lords" with which the little barrister laced every conversation.

"Oh, it will, my lord. You must give it time, but remember, this is the land of your birth. Given time . . ."

"Given time, Norton, I will be returning to my home in the United States," said Jared firmly, his hard stare daring Norton to question the location of his home since New Orleans, by agreement with the judge, was now off-limits to the new Marquess Winter.

"If you say so, my lord. I want to thank you for looking after me these past weeks. I apologize for being so ill."

"I told you, I didn't mind. Let's just say I was repaying you for getting me out of prison."

"I was never really clear on one thing, my lord," Norton said. "Why did Judge Crenshaw hate you so?"

"Well, there was the matter of his daughter." Jared grinned.

"My lord! I trust she was not . . ."

"No, no, nothing like that. The real reason goes back a few years. Crenshaw accused me of helping the enemy—that would be the British—during the war."

"And were you?" asked Norton, before saying hastily, "I beg your pardon, my lord. That is none of my business!"

"As a matter of fact, no, I wasn't. But I was looking into the problem of someone sending secrets to the enemy. I suspected Crenshaw, but I couldn't prove it. His daughter let slip something. . . . The war is over now, but I think Crenshaw has been worried I might soil his reputation."

"Dirty business, spying," said Norton.

"Just so. But tell me something of your England," said Jared, turning his back to the distant shoreline and facing the solicitor.

"Just wait until you see London, my lord. Just wait. It is a wonderful city, a very old city. The buildings are very fine, and we have some of the most beautiful homes in the world. Your own town house is reputed to be one of the most beautiful, my lord, with very graceful proportions."

"What of the ladies, Norton?" Jared leered at the captain's wife, who was simpering at him from nearby.

The solicitor's blush made Jared smile. But Norton said sensibly, "I suppose the ladies are no more beautiful in London than they are in New Orleans, but they are very refined and very elegant."

"You could be speaking of the architecture again, Norton. What about their, you know, talents?"

"Really, my lord!" protested the little man, tugging at his cravat.

"Never mind, Norton. I was being facetious. I have no doubt the ladies are wonderful. How long will it take to get to London once we dock in Portsmouth? I'm anxious to meet them."

Suddenly, Norton's cravat appeared ready to strangle him, and he coughed and sputtered for a full minute while Jared gazed at him with narrowed eyes.

Finally, gasping for air, he said hoarsely, "A few days, to be sure. But of course, you will be wanting to rest after this arduous voyage, my lord."

"I feel fine, Norton. Ready for anything. But perhaps I'm speaking prematurely. What is it you haven't told me? That bit about the fortune—does the debt perhaps outweigh it?"

"Now, now, my lord, nothing like that, I assure you," said Norton, smiling again. He cleared his throat and gave his cravat another tug. "It is just that I thought, you see, I would be bringing back a lad, a youth of fifteen or sixteen."

"So? Surely that makes no difference." There was no humor lurking in the icy blue eyes now.

"Yes, well, there is one problem. When I thought you were your brother . . . that is, I thought the new marquess would be your brother . . ."

"Out with it," snapped Jared.

"It is just that I engaged a tutor for you, my lord, someone to help you with social and political issues, perhaps even"—Norton's voice fell—"elocution."

Jared's smile rapidly turned into a guffaw, and the solicitor breathed a sigh of relief.

"You don't know how relieved I am to know you are not offended, my lord," said Norton with a wheezing chuckle. "I was much concerned you might be insulted when I revealed what I had done. It has been weighing heavily on my mind."

"Why should I be insulted, Norton? You had no way of knowing. You can let this tutor know he is no longer needed, and everything will be fine."

"But, my lord!" exclaimed Norton.

"Don't worry, Norton. I will see that the fellow is well compensated for his trouble." When this statement didn't relieve the solicitor's discomfiture, Jared added impatiently, "I assume I can afford a month or two of salary for the poor fellow."

"As to that, my lord, you could afford a lifetime of salaries for a tutor, but . . . well . . ."

"Go on," came the ominous prod.

"It is just, my lord . . . that is, I feel, my lord . . . there is the matter of your seat in the House of Lords, my lord. You will have to make your maiden speech. A tutor could be of immeasurable service to you, to your . . . that is, while your present speech is very colorful and your education obviously more than adequate, well, when one is a peer of the realm, my lord . . ." Norton's suffering ended under the new marquess's stabbing scowl.

"You think the new marquess, being from the backwaters of New Orleans, won't fit in with London's . . . how did my father refer to it?—*ton?*"

"Indeed, my lord, it is not . . ."

"I've a good mind to take the next ship back and bedamned to you and the inheritance!"

Jared turned on his heel and strolled away, his casual gait belying his fury. How dare the little weasel! Of all the arrogance! If he had been fifteen, if Willie had survived that monstrous attack instead. . . .

Jared gazed across the open sea, breathing slowly and carefully to control his frustration. He couldn't very well return to New Orleans before he had received something for his trouble. Oh, he would return home. He certainly had no intention of becoming a London dandy. But he would remain only until he could plunder the estate, sell it, give it away . . . anything to be rid of the damnable millstone!

"Mr. Winter? Or should I say Lord Winter?" giggled the captain's wife. "I heard about your good fortune, my lord. You must be thrilled!"

He turned toward the sultry tones of Mrs. Fox, but his expression was less than friendly.

"What may I do for you, ma'am?" he said, his drawl more pronounced than ever.

"I wondered if you would be staying in London? I

was thinking of visiting my sister for a month or two. She resides near London now."

"I really don't know what my plans are at this time, Mrs. Fox."

"Of course, my lord, of course," she simpered, coyly gazing at his broad chest before looking up and smiling again. "My husband will be taking another shipment of goods back to New Orleans immediately, and I'm afraid I will be terribly lonely without him."

"Then I suggest you make the return trip with him. Good day, Mrs. Fox."

With that, Jared returned to his cabin, locking the door behind him. The last thing he wanted was another round of Norton's justifications. He threw himself onto the bed. Raising his arms and lacing his hands beneath his head, he stared at the ceiling.

What the devil could he do? He didn't want the blasted title, but the money . . . not that he felt it was due to him. There were probably some very deserving tenants and stewards who had been looking after the estate for years who deserved it more than he, a stranger, a foreigner.

He closed his eyes, and his father's image floated past. Not the man he had become, a worn, hardened farmer, but the laughing figure Jared remembered from his childhood, before the years of toil and frustrated failures had silenced his laughter.

When Willie was born, they were happy, all four of them. They had homesteaded in the territory northwest of New Orleans. Mama and Father, they laughed all the time then. And Willie . . . there had never been a sweeter little boy. He had spent his days riding on

Jared's shoulders or mounted behind the saddle on Jared's pony. Jared had been content for a time.

Then he had told his parents he was going back to New Orleans for a month or two. The farm, he told them, wasn't interesting enough. It wasn't exciting enough. And he had ridden away. His last memory of his parents and brother was of them smiling, waving, and crying.

When he returned two months later, the ruins of their cabin were still smoking. Their closest neighbors were digging the graves and building the coffins.

It had been years since he had allowed himself to remember. The guilt had been unbearable, though he knew if he had been there, the outcome wouldn't have changed. He would have died with his family. Tears slid past his temples, unheeded and unchecked.

No, he thought, sitting up and slamming his fist against the wall. He didn't deserve this inheritance, but his father had. Willie had. His mother had. And for them, he would take it. He would prove to all the self-righteous, supercilious Englishmen what it really meant to be a man, a marquess.

With his jaw set and his nostrils flared, he left the small cabin, climbed the stairs and rejoined Norton by the rail.

"I will take care of this tutor," he said, his voice as haughty as that as the highest stickler in the *ton*. "If you have anymore surprises for me, tell me now."

"None, my lord," said the solicitor. He smiled but refrained from rubbing his hands in glee.

Three

When lovely woman stoops to folly,
And finds too late that men betray,
What charm can soothe her melancholy?
What art can wash her tears away?
                                    —Oliver Goldsmith

Lady Henrietta, sister to the Duke of Bosworth, wiped her damp brow, arched her back, and stretched her tired muscles before returning to her work on the cluttered table in her sitting room. After a few moments, her out-of-tune humming ceased, and she put down the piece of steel wool and the curved piece of wood, shaking her head.

"It is no use, Penny. I will go blind if I continue to work by candlelight," she said, dusting off her hands and closing the large armoire. "And by tomorrow, I will be much too busy with my new pupil to worry with my little obsession. This one will have to wait, probably until we return home again."

She left her sitting room, the diminutive foxhound

on her heels, and entered her bedroom. It was not as spacious as her quarters in her own house, but it was comfortable. When she had learned that the house Tobias Norton had selected for the marquess Winter's school was unfurnished, Hetty had transferred her personal furnishings into the bedchamber and sitting room she had selected for her own use.

The largest chamber and sitting room would belong to the young marquess, as was only fitting. No sense, she had thought, in wasting time getting down to business. The young man needed to know that in this society, a marquess was miles above a mere tutor, especially when she kept her counsel about her family title and connections.

Hetty had carefully selected the furnishings for the marquess's room, debating for many hours over the blue or red velvet draperies and the choice of furniture. In the end, she had chosen the royal blue counterpane and bed curtains. The color, she felt, helped brighten the dark, heavy pieces of furniture which Mr. Norton's clerk had insisted were *de rigueur* for a marquess. She had insisted, however, that the size of the bed be normal, warning the clerk that a boy from the country would feel too lonely in a huge bed such as the clerk wanted. He had acquiesced, and peace had settled over the new house in Audley Street as they awaited the master's arrival.

Hetty glanced at the clock on the mantle. She knew her nerves were on edge. It was already two o'clock in the morning, and she was still wide awake. The marquess, according to Mr. Norton's note, would arrive on the morrow, and she was going to be exhausted.

"You are lucky, Penny. You can sleep all day. I will look like a hag and feel wretched as well."

The little dog, half the size of a normal foxhound, was another of Hetty's projects. Ten years ago, she had rescued this runt of the litter from drowning at the hands of the huntmaster. Penny sat up on her hind legs, wagged her tail, and happily accepted the stale biscuit left from evening tea. Hetty picked up the solicitor's note and reread it for the twentieth time.

Dear Miss Thompson,
    We have arrived in Portsmouth and will journey overland to London tomorrow. I will bring the marquess to Audley Street on the second of February.

                                            Your servant,
                                            Tobias Norton

"You see, it is written by a man, Penny," said Hetty, holding the letter out for the little dog to see. "He gives me no information—no idea of the boy's personality, character, not even a physical description. It could have been written about a statue. He does not even tell me if the boy is fifteen or sixteen. Is he educated, as Mr. Norton assumed, or is he completely uncivilized—and therefore, I might add, completely unsuitable to become the great Marquess Winter?"

The dog jumped into her lap, turning round and round before settling down for a snooze. Stroking Penny's smooth head, Hetty sighed.

"Whatever he is, we will do our best," she said.

She picked up a beautifully carved lyre and strummed on it expertly for a few seconds before her voice joined in. Her singing was neither as expert nor as beautiful as her playing, but Hetty put every ounce of emotion into her off-key rendition of "Barbra Allen."

Some time later, she laid the instrument aside and sighed. She was looking forward to this challenge; her life had become monotonous. Her eyes drooped closed and her breathing became even and shallow.

"I know it is late, Norton, but devil take me if I'll spend another night in an inn curled up in some cramped bed. I long to stretch out and sleep like a man instead of a pretzel!"

"Please, my lord! Tomorrow would be much better," protested the solicitor, trying to come between his tall client and the front door.

Before Jared could push past the solicitor, the door opened slowly, and a frail frame, feet hastily stuffed into slippers and black coat dragged on over a nightshirt, was outlined by the candlelight from beyond.

"Ah, Mr. Norton, you have arrived early. We were expecting you tomorrow."

"Yes, thank you, uh . . ."

"Sanders, sir."

"Yes, Sanders. We are sorry to disturb the house this late, but his lordship was impatient to reach our destination."

"Think nothing of it. Come in, come in," said

Hetty's most proper butler, his sharp old eyes quickly masking surprise when the new Marquess Winter stepped into the light, filling the threshold with his large frame.

"Welcome, my lord," Sanders said formally, bowing so deeply Jared had to steady him when he lost his balance. "Thank you. Sanders, is it? I hope there is some food to be had. I am famished. And if there is not yet a fire in my room, please see to it at once."

"Very good, my lord. I will rouse the cook, and there is already a small fire in your room, but I will have the footman build it up to help take away the chill."

Jared dropped his guise as the haughty lord and smiled at the old servant. "Thank you, Sanders. I guess I was so anxious to arrive I didn't stop and think how very inconvenient my appearance at this hour would be for all of you. Tell the cook to send up anything, please."

Jared turned to Norton, placing a hand on his shoulder. "I imagine you would like to seek your own bed, Tobias. I will see you tomorrow afternoon, perhaps. Until then, good night, and thank you." He shook the surprised solicitor's limp hand and turned to follow the footman up the stairs.

"Wha . . . ?" Hetty sat up and blinked rapidly as she looked around the room to discover what had disturbed her slumber. Penny deserted her lap and trotted to the bed, hopping onto a soft pillow and curling up again.

Hetty rubbed her eyes and stood, shrugging out of her wrapper. Then she heard a thud and a mumbled curse. Frowning, she slipped into the old wrapper, tying it tightly around her waist as she peeked out the door. The firelight coming from the marquess's future room was inordinately bright.

Fire! She threw open the door and rushed down the short corridor, her bare feet making no sound. When she pushed the door fully open, it collided with the buttocks of the present marquess, who jumped straight up.

"What the devil? Blast this infernal thing!" Still dancing on one foot, Jared whirled around and snapped, "Who the hell are you? Oh, never mind! Help me get this cursed boot off!"

Speechless, Hetty complied, her eyes widening when he plopped into the chair, took her hand, spun her around, and planted his stockinged foot on her backside. Without considering her action, she took his raised, booted foot in both hands and tugged. The offending boot came off suddenly, sending her careening toward the fire. Strong hands encircled her waist, preventing her from falling headlong into the flames, and she turned to find herself staring into the bluest eyes she had ever seen. She resisted the instinct to pat her hair—which was hopelessly disordered—into place.

Taking a step backward, and then another, she said breathlessly, "Only tell me you are not my new pupil!"

"Watch out!" Jared again pulled her away from the flames.

"Oh, thank you," she said, dropping her gaze before

adding belatedly, "my lord." Hetty dropped an elegant curtsy, the action bordering on the absurd considering her state of undress.

Jared looked down at the floor, studying it to give himself time to think. Pupil? If this was the tutor Norton had told him about . . . well, perhaps it wasn't such a bad thing.

"I'm sorry, my lord. I should introduce myself. I am Miss Thompson." She smoothed her worn wrapper and wished she liked frills instead of comfort. Extending her hand, she added, in what she hoped was a kindly manner, "I believe Mr. Norton has probably misled both of us. I was expecting someone much younger."

Jared shuffled his feet and shook his head, mumbling an incoherent reply.

Perhaps, thought Hetty, *the man is a simpleton and has mastered only obscenities.* Still, her motherly instincts rushed to the fore, and she spoke, using the same tone her nurse had used whenever she was ill. "I realize this is a strange place, my lord. But we will soon have you used to it and our strange ways. Mr. Norton did tell you about me, didn't he?"

Jared nodded.

"Good. Then you must know I am here to help you in any way I can. I hope we can be friends."

Why, she thinks I'm some kind of fool, probably because I am a colonial, thought Jared indignantly. *If a man isn't English. . . . Of all the condescending females! Well, we'll just see about that!*

Jared hid the twinkle in his eyes, replacing it with

a nervous twitch and slack-jawed expression before looking up at his new tutor.

"Yes'm. I reckon as how yer gonna be my teacher lady. Thank'ee." For good measure, he pulled on his hair and bobbed a submissive bow.

Hetty blinked and gave him a forced smile. "Why, you're very welcome. Really, this is most irregular, our meeting like this. You must be exhausted after your journey. I will let you get some sleep."

"Thank'ee, ma'am. Night."

"Good night, my lord," said Hetty, sketching a slight curtsy before stepping into the corridor and closing the door.

She returned to her room, removed the offensive wrapper, and joined Penny on the bed. "Some guard you are," she said, scratching the hound's ear absent-mindedly. "I have met our newest pupil, and he is most interesting.

"The only words I understood were unsuitable to repeat," she whispered to her four-legged confidante. "A shame, too. He is so very handsome.

"Not that it matters, not at all! But the young ladies will be sorely put out when they discover the new marquess is dim-witted." Despite herself, Hetty giggled.

"I suppose, though, I should reserve judgment until I have spoken to Mr. Norton, don't you think, Penny?" The little dog yawned and stretched, wriggling out of Hetty's reach.

"Very well, I will let you go back to sleep. I just want you to know that, should I decide to stay, it's going to be a very long winter."

* * *

"Mr. Norton! Just the man I wanted to see!" exclaimed Hetty, descending the stairs the next morning just as Sanders opened the front door.

"Miss Thompson, how good to see you again. I'm sorry my client was so insistent about coming last night. I hope his arrival didn't disturb you."

Hetty opened her mouth to speak, then decided her initial encounter with the slow-witted marquess was best kept secret. With her head high, she entered the formal salon, and the solicitor followed her nervously.

When she was seated, she said, "We did meet briefly, Mr. Norton, but it was only long enough for me to realize Lord Winter is hardly a boy!"

"I must apologize, Miss Thompson. My information was incorrect, of course. It seems the first son, this man, did not die on the voyage to America as an infant. Instead, the second son, his brother, the one who would have been sixteen or so, was killed by roving marauders when he was only a wee boy—not that his death makes any difference, since the present marquess is some fifteen years older than his brother was and would have been the one to inherit regardless."

"Marauders! How dreadful!" gasped Hetty, her fertile imagination supplying horrific details about such a tragedy. She favored the solicitor with a frown for his callous speech.

"Of course, of course. It was a tragedy, but for our purposes . . ." The solicitor wilted beneath her glacial stare and continued haltingly, "You understand what I mean, Miss Thompson."

"Yes, yes, but back to the matter at hand, Mr. Norton. Why did you not say in the note you sent to me from Portsmouth that the new marquess was a grown man, much too mature to need a woman's instruction?"

Tobias Norton thought the new marquess would be much more likely to tolerate, even enjoy, receiving his lessons from a woman, and would probably be happy to give a few to Miss Thompson on certain matters, but he kept his own counsel about that.

Instead, shaking his head, he said, "On the contrary, Miss Thompson, I believe Lord Winter is more needful of your help than ever. Oh, I grant you, he can be charming in a rustic sort of way, but he will have no idea how to go on in the Polite World."

"But, Mr. Norton, surely a man would be better for this task," said Hetty.

"I can't agree, Miss Thompson. I doubt the marquess would accept such an arrangement. And only think, unless you help, he must enter Society as an adult without any preparation, and without the excuse for his behavior and his language, I might add, which a child might be granted. He will be crucified, to put it succinctly."

Hetty shook her head and rose, moving to the window which overlooked the street. Even in this quiet neighborhood, there was the occasional fancy equipage, the dandy strolling home after a late night on the town. She slipped behind the curtain as a passing gentleman tipped his hat to her.

"You know I am right," he said quietly.

London society was an unkind being, fueled as it

was by gossip and scandal. The new marquess was no more than a babe in the woods. The gentlemen would probably blackball him from the clubs, and the scheming mamas would shortly have him bound up with a shrewish wife who cared only for her own pleasure and would gladly suffer being wed to a rustic for the privilege.

There had been—she couldn't bring the right word to mind, but something—in those eyes which had appealed to her. Not romantically, of course, but as a fellow—what was the word she searched for? *Misfit,* perhaps?

"Very well," she finally replied, turning back to Norton and shaking her head again. "But you must talk to him, tell him exactly why I am here. I fear he doesn't completely understand. I only hope he will not be too offended. Of course, last night he didn't seem too surprised by my presence."

"So you did speak to him?"

"Only briefly, as I said."

"And what was your impression of him?" asked the solicitor eagerly. He had every confidence Jared could charm any lady, even a strict schoolmistress like Miss Thompson.

"He was not very vocal."

"The marquess?" asked Norton in wonder.

"Yes, I fear it will take a great deal of work to ready him for his place in Society."

"Really?"

Hetty read his surprise as apprehension and said hurriedly, "Do not despair, Mr. Norton. There are many in the *ton* who are . . ." She had planned to say "slow-tops," but decided this would not have a calming effect on the nervous little solicitor, and finished with, "not as clever as others. That should not concern you overly. And, after all, you are here to look after his estate's business, so he will have no concerns financially. But it will take a great deal of work to make Lord Winter into a marquess who can pass muster in the *ton*. I will certainly do my best, but I can make no promises."

"I'm certain you will, Miss Thompson," said Tobias Norton. "But tell me, did you not find Lord Winter charming? Presentable?"

"He is quite handsome, I suppose, but charming? Perhaps, upon closer acquaintance, I will discover in him a sort of simple charm."

"I see."

"I will inquire if his lordship has risen and have him sent to you here so you may explain to him, in the simplest possible terms, why I am here. Good day, Mr. Norton."

"Good day, Miss Thompson." He rose as she left the room.

Moments later, Jared, Marquess Winter, entered the neat salon, put a finger to his lips, and grinned, shutting the door behind him.

"Good morning, Tobias," he said, crossing the room and slapping the solicitor on the back. "Sanders said you wanted to see me. Ah, here is breakfast. I told him to serve it in here. You'll join me, of course."

The footman placed the heavy tray on a low table, and Jared pulled a chair close, signaling to the solicitor to do the same. Norton, however, stayed where he was, frowning suspiciously at his employer.

After a moment, Jared looked up, mouth full, and mumbled, "I do wish you would cease hovering over me like some kind of vulture."

"I'm sorry, my lord," said the solicitor, still frowning, but joining Jared. He accepted a cup of coffee but waved away the plate of food.

"You have met Miss Thompson," Norton said.

"Yes, interesting young woman. Helped me get my boot off last night. My foot had swollen, I suppose, from riding in that blasted carriage all day and night. You really should have allowed me to ride, you know. I mean, no one need have known who I was, and I would have been much more comfortable." When Jared could no longer tolerate the solicitor's fixed stare, he demanded, "What is it?"

"She . . . took . . . off . . . your . . . boot?"

"Why, yes. I didn't know who she was at the time, of course, but she came into my room. What now?"

"She . . . came . . . into . . . your . . ."

"Cut line, man! I didn't ravish her!"

"Well, no, I never . . . it is just that a lady would never, should never . . . perhaps I have been mistaken in bringing her here. If she would . . ."

"But she didn't!" Jared pushed away from the food. "See what you've done? I've completely lost my appetite."

"I'm sorry, my lord. But I am coming to realize this is a mistake. Miss Thompson came to me under protest, but she had the highest recommendations, and I was absolutely certain having her here to teach you how to go on would be perfectly reasonable. I had no idea she would be party to such impropriety! My lord, I must make other arrangements. If anyone were to discover you and Miss Thompson here, together . . ."

"Nonsense, Tobias." Jared smiled at the nervous little man. "Miss Thompson and I, I feel certain, will get along very well. As a matter of fact, I can't think of anyone else more suitable to the job of teaching me how I need to go on."

"But, my lord, you cannot be thinking properly. You cannot treat Miss Thompson as if she were a servant or some boon companion, asking her to help you undress!" he said, wiping his brow and shaking his head vigorously. "And she, if she were a lady, would not allow it!"

"Look, Norton, it was a mistake. She came in, probably thinking a servant was working late, and found me stumbling around, trying to dislodge that demmed boot. Of course she offered to help," said Jared, his blue eyes entreating the solicitor to relax while his mind recalled the way Miss Thompson had felt when he had grabbed her waist and turned her in his arms to save her from falling. There was something about a woman unrestricted by corsets that set his senses reeling.

Clearing his throat, Jared added sensibly, "It will not happen again."

"Are you certain, my lord?"

"Swear it on my uncle's grave."

Norton raised a bushy brow reprovingly, but relented enough to say, "Very well. I suppose I will have to trust you. It would be impossible to find anyone else."

"Thank you for having such faith in me, Tobias. Now, if you will excuse me, I believe I will see Miss Thompson about setting up a schedule for my lessons. I doubt the nursery would be well suited to our needs." Jared rose and moved quickly toward the door, hoping to make his escape before the solicitor could recall some other objection.

"There is one other enigma, my lord," said Norton, his eyes narrowing as he studied his employer's reaction.

But Jared, who was accustomed to bluffing his way through the toughest card games against the most hardened gamester, merely regarded the other man with polite interest, making the solicitor twitch nervously.

"Miss Thompson appears to have the impression you are less than intelligent. I must wonder how she arrived at such an erroneous conclusion. She does not appear the sort who would make such a determination without reason, my lord."

"I did notice there was something in her expression when she looked at me. I suppose she feels any man of thirty who requires a tutor must not be very shrewd," said Jared, frowning thoughtfully.

"There is that."

"And of course, she is probably thinking of all the tedious details, social details, which she must drill into my head before I am ready for my presentation to London Society."

"Perhaps," said Norton, beginning to relax again.

"And then there is my horrendous accent, you know. She no doubt realizes it will take hours and hours of practice before I can be taught proper elocution. Really, I am amazed she agreed to such an onerous task."

Norton frowned again, and Jared recognized that he had gone a little too far with his justification. It wouldn't do for the little man to spoil the game at this point. He had given up everything he loved—if one forgot about the hangman's noose—to accept this inheritance. The least he could get out of it was a bit of fun with a haughty, dried-up, spinster schoolmistress.

"But I'll do my best, Tobias." Jared patted the older man on the shoulder and ushered him out the door.

He returned to the tray and downed several bites of egg before the door to the salon opened again.

The haughty, dried-up spinster entered, curtsied, and smiled.

Dried up?

In a glance, Jared took in the shapely figure, modestly gowned, and proceeded to choke on the egg. It splattered across the tray while Miss Thompson rushed to his side and began beating on his back.

When he waved her away, she asked, "Are you quite all right, my lord? Here, take this." She poured him a glass of water which he downed in two gulps, his face red and his throat raw.

"Better?" she asked, taking the glass from his hands and smiling again.

He nodded and said hoarsely, "Yes'm, thank 'ee."

"Thank *you*," she corrected gently, tugging the bellpull. "Sanders, have this cleared away. Lord Winter and I will be working in the study this morning. Please see we are not disturbed."

"Very good, miss," said the butler. He raised a brow as Jared, his blue eyes twinkling, followed Hetty from the room.

"I hope she knows what she's doing," muttered the old family retainer, frowning sternly when the footman grinned at him. "Take this tray back to the kitchen, lad. Then clean the carpet."

"Of course, Mr. Sanders."

The footman hurried to do the butler's bidding, and Sanders turned and followed his mistress to the study.

She was standing on a stool, selecting a book from the shelves while the marquess eyed her trim ankles appreciatively.

Clearly his throat rather loudly, the butler asked, "Will you be needing anything else, miss?"

Hetty turned to answer and lost her balance. Jared sprang forward, averting her fall, a fact which appeared to gratify the marquess greatly as he caught her around the waist.

"Oh, I do apologize, my lord," Hetty said breathlessly as he set her feet firmly on the floor again.

"Think nothin' of it, miss," said Jared, hanging his head bashfully.

Sanders cleared his throat again.

"Oh, Sanders. No, no, we are fine. Just see we are not disturbed, please."

"Of course, miss."

Hetty straightened her green morning gown and glanced in the mirror over the fireplace. "Oh dear. My hair looks a fright. If you'll excuse me, my lord,

I will go and make myself presentable again. This hair of mine." Hetty swept past him, wondering why she continued to prattle on, but unable to stop her inane chatter. "It's so soft, I can't get it to stay in place properly."

"It's right purty, miss," said Jared, smiling shyly until she was out of the room.

Was this the same woman who had come to his rescue last night? He must have been more sleepy than he thought! She might be a spinster, but how he could have thought of her as dried up, he couldn't imagine. She wasn't a beauty, of course, but she was pretty, with lovely eyes. And her figure! Those were the sort of curves in which a man could lose himself.

He smiled, wondering what color her eyes were and if his very proper teacher might be persuaded into bed with her rather mature, decidedly improper pupil. Persuading her would certainly make his visit more enjoyable.

"I thought you might like more coffee, my lord," said Sanders, carrying in a small tray and sitting it on the desk. "And I have brought some tea for Miss Thompson."

The servant took in the empty room, turning to Jared and frowning as if the butler suspected him of having devoured the lady in question.

"She has gone upstairs to fix her hair," Jared explained.

Sanders trudged toward the door, but paused before leaving to say, "Yes, my mistress always likes to look neat and proper. Very proper." Old eyes met blue and held.

"Your mistress will come to no harm from me, Sanders. Word of a Winter," said Jared, echoing the phrase his father had been so fond of saying.

Sanders studied the marquess for a moment before nodding and saying, "Very good, my lord." Then he toddled away.

Jared took a sip of the hot liquid and burned his tongue, letting fly a colorful curse. "Damn that butler," he muttered.

So much for corrupting Miss Thompson, he thought with a sigh. Still, there would be no harm in teaching her a little about Americans, without stepping over the line. Surely she was old enough to allow a man to tread on that line somewhat.

As Miss Thompson entered, Jared looked up and gave a soft whistle. She appeared startled and blushed a most delectable shade of pink.

Yes, he could teach her one or two things.

Four

Oh, what a tangled web we weave,
When first we practice to deceive . . .
— *Sir Walter Scott*

"Now, my lord, would you please read this passage I have marked?" Hetty handed him a slim volume of essays.

Jared turned the book over and glanced at the cover. He scanned the selected paragraph before beginning. It was a book for children, the vocabulary quite rudimentary.

She doesn't have a high opinion of my intellect, he thought with a grimace. *Very well then, I will do my best to live down to her expectations.*

"If you would prefer, you may simply read the first sentence, and I will read the next," said Hetty, mistaking his hesitation.

"I kin do it." Jared slouched in the chair, resting the open book on his chest and frowning as if the task at hand took a great deal of concentration.

"Th' young lad ran acrosst the medder."

Hetty smiled brightly as she interrupted, "Very good, my lord."

"Y' know, ma'am, I sure would like it ifn' you'd call me Jared. I never took t' school much, an' you callin' me 'my lord' all the time surely takes me back t' somethin' I'd rather not remember, y' know."

"But it is your title, and hearing me use it will help you grow accustomed to it, my lord," said Hetty.

"I dunno. It just makes me remember that teacher I had back home. She musta been a hunnert years old, and she had this hideous wart on th' side o' her nose." Jared paused, scrutinizing Hetty's clear, smooth complexion with the eye of a connoisseur. "At least you don't have no wart, but I surely wish you'd call me Jared, just t' make me feel better."

"It would be highly irregular," Hetty hedged. He looked so pitiful, she relented and said quickly, "Very well. I don't see it will do any harm. After all, you are much older than my other pupils have been." She flushed a dull red and added, "I beg your pardon, my lord. That was very maladroit—poorly done."

"Aw, shucks, ma'am, don't think anything of it. If I can't take a little kiddin' . . ."

"Kitten?" Hetty frowned in a most diverting manner.

"Kiddin'," he reiterated. "Y' know, teasing?"

"Oh, I see. It must be an American expression."

"That's right. I'm afraid I got lots of 'em."

"Yes, yes, well, we will soon set you to rights. Oh! There, I did it again. Please forgive me. I didn't mean to imply your language—your dialect, that is—needs to be set to rights, my lord."

Jared allowed the laugh that had been building to burst forth, and Hetty soon joined in. Her eyes, he noticed, turned a warm brown when she was amused. Or perhaps it was the way she lifted her head, the sunlight catching the color and illuminating those dark eyes from within.

"Let's begin again, Jared," Hetty said when she had sufficiently recovered.

"Done!" Jared took the book in hand and read slowly, as if with painstaking effort. "The young lad ran across the medder."

"Meadow," said Hetty. "Very good. Now read the next."

"The sun was as bright and purty as a jon . . . I don't believe I've ever seen that word before, miss."

"Jonquil. It is a yellow flower. Perhaps you know it as a daffodil. In the spring, my garden at home will be full of them. They bloom quite early in the season. I love them."

"I know what you mean. They're a welcome sight after a long winter. What are the winters like around here?" he asked, letting the book close.

"Quite cold at times, but there is the occasional pretty day, even in winter."

"Not too pretty here in London, I don't guess," said Jared, admiring the way her green gown rose and fell over her ample curves. "Too many people and gray buildings."

"Oh, we have parks that are quite pretty, especially

in the spring. Of course, they are rather crowded at certain times of the day."

"Why is that?"

"Well, people go there to stroll down the lanes, to ride on horseback, or take a drive," explained Hetty, pacifying her sense of dedication with the knowledge that the marquess needed social guidance every bit as much as he needed elocution lessons.

"If all these people like the parks so much, why don't they live in the country?" Jared asked, forgetting his accent completely. Hetty didn't appear to notice, and he breathed a sigh of relief.

"There are other reasons for going to the park, Jared." Hetty paused, but he said nothing, only tilting his head to one side—rather, she thought, like her hound Penny. "They go to the park, especially Rotten Row in Hyde Park, to see and be seen."

"By whom?"

"Each other. It is a place to socialize, to make the acquaintance of new people."

"So if I see some pretty young lady I want to meet, I can just go to the park and start talkin' to her?"

"Oh, no, that would not be proper! You would need to arrange to have someone introduce you first. Then you could speak to her," said Hetty hurriedly.

Jared shook his head, saying, "Seems a mighty peculiar way to go about things, miss. Or can I call you Henrietta?"

"Why, I . . ." Hetty reflected briefly that it surely couldn't hurt, and such a familiar form of address might help him feel more comfortable. Finally, she said emphatically, "You may *not* call me Henrietta, ever. But you may call me Hetty when we are alone together. When there is anyone about, even the servants, you must call me Miss Thompson."

"I see," said Jared, shaking his head again to indicate he didn't see at all, thought Hetty. "Y'all set a great store by such things here, don't ya?"

"Yes, I'm afraid we do. Now, we must return to our other lessons," she said, indicating he should open the book.

"The hosses . . ."

"Jared?"

"Yes, Hetty?" he said.

Bemused, Hetty lost her train of thought for a moment. How odd it was to hear a man, an extremely attractive man, call her by her Christian name. Why, until she had insisted, even Perry Bigglesby had only ventured to call her Miss Hetty.

The silence had held for too long to be comfortable. Hoping to mask her reverie, she cleared her throat.

"Do ya want I should pound yer back?"

"No, no, that won't be necessary," she said quickly when Jared started to rise.

Jared sat on the edge of the chair, his hands on his knees, elbows bent, and his neck jutting forward. His head lolled to one side as though the effort to keep it upright was beyond his capabilities.

"I always say, Jared, we must begin as we mean to go on. First, before you speak, you must be seated properly. Sit up straight with both feet on the floor. Good. Now, straighten your shoulders and look me in the eye, Jared," said the schoolmistress.

He complied.

"Very nice. You will find this posture much more conducive—more suitable, that is—to speech, whether you are reading or conversing."

"Do you want I should read again?"

"Yes, please continue."

Jared continued until he had finished the page. Hetty interrupted from time to time, correcting some of his more glaring mistakes in pronunciation, but she was pleased he could decipher the words properly. At least she wouldn't have to teach him to read.

By the time the butler announced a light luncheon, Jared was thoroughly sick of his chosen roll as country bumpkin. He grinned as he heard Hetty's sigh of relief. Judging by the eager manner in which his teacher jumped up, she was also finding this session on pronunciation a trial. Jared leaped to his feet, beating her to the door.

"Jared," she said, her tone a reproof.

"Yes, He . . . Miss Thompson?" he said, altering his form of address when she cocked a brow in the direction of Sanders.

"A gentleman does not race a lady to the door. He always rises in a stately manner and offers a lady his arm."

"Why? Can't she git where she's goin' without it?"

"No, because it is the polite thing to do. Now that you are a marquess, you must do the polite thing at all times."

Jared stuck out his elbow and Hetty lightly placed her hand on it as they walked the short distance to the small dining room.

Hetty could feel the heat of his body through the

cloth of his jacket. *At least,* she thought, *he is clean.* She could not bear to be so close to a man who had never been introduced to a bar of soap. It was quite odd, really, he would be so well groomed and yet so uncouth in speech and behavior.

As if reading her mind, Jared asked, "Do you like my new clothes? Mr. Norton—ain't he a nice gentleman?—saw to it I had 'em afore we left New Orleans," he lied. "Made me promise if I was to have 'em, I'd keep myself as neat as a pin. I've kept my word, too!" he added proudly, sticking out his chin for her inspection. "And I've shaved every day since then, even on that boat!"

"That is commendable, my lord, and you look very nice. Until you mentioned it, it hadn't occurred to me we should send for the tailor. You will need a complete wardrobe," said Hetty. Then she turned scarlet and begged his pardon.

"I shouldn't have spoken to you about such an intimate matter, my lord."

"Wasn't anything, miss. You know better than me about such things. Stands to reason."

"You are very understanding, my lord," she said formally. "Here we are. Now, you must escort me to my chair, pull it out for me, since there is no footman in attendance to do so, and push it in when I am seated."

"Argh!" Hetty pushed away from the polished table seconds later. "Not quite so energetically, Jared."

"I'm right sorry, miss," he said, grinning behind her back.

He ignored the place setting at the far end of the table, taking the chair beside hers.

Hetty said patiently, "No, you should take the chair on the opposite end."

"Why? There's no one else to fill up these empty places. We might as well be comfortable. Or do you want we should have to shout at each other?" commented Jared.

"Oh, very well. I will move my place to your end of the table. This is your house and your table. You should be seated at the head of it. Sanders, please see to it the place settings are changed."

"Doesn't feel like my table," Jared grumbled. "Feels like yours."

When they were alone again, Hetty remarked, "You must tell me if you dislike any of the furnishings, Jared. I assumed, as you know, the new marquess would be little more than a boy and, as such, would have no interest in the running of the household. But it is your house, and we can change the furniture, the draperies, and so on. I chose what I liked and what I thought would suit this house."

"No, no, the house is fine. Almost everything in it is, too, except . . ."

"Yes, what is it?"

"That bed of mine! There I am, curled up like a pretzel, trying to sleep. I don't think I kin take much more of it!"

"A pretzel? What do you mean, a pretzel?" she asked, with no slight degree of trepidation.

"It's kind of a bread thing, a dough, but not soft. The monks used to make them, back a hundred years or two. They're all folded up to look like a child praying. Anyway, that's what I feel like in that tiny bed."

"I suppose I should have listened to the clerk." Hetty frowned.

"The clerk?"

"Yes. Mr. Norton's man chose a bed that was simply huge, much too large for a boy, and I told him it was unsuitable."

"Huge?" he said wistfully. "You have no idea, Hetty, how nice it would be to cover up under that counterpane all stretched out, without my feet and arms falling off the bed."

"I will contact Mr. Norton today. You will have your new bed by tomorrow night. I am sorry."

"There's no reason to be, Hetty. You couldn't know I was going to be so tall and long-legged."

"You are too kind," she murmured, blushing and trying to erase the image from her mind of strong, bare legs and arms escaping everywhere. Judging from what she had seen of him in his shirt sleeves the night before, there were broad, muscled shoulders to match.

The dining room felt suddenly warm, and Hetty hastened to change the subject. "Tell me about your schooling, Jared. Surely your father sent you to school."

"There wasn't much money for that sort of thing, so my mother taught me to read, and Father taught me some Latin and Greek and sums, of course."

"Indeed, that is most impressive. I'm afraid I know almost no Latin or Greek."

"Why not? Didn't your parents send you to school?" Jared couldn't resist the opportunity to tease her.

"Of course, but being a girl, I learned to play the

harp and pianoforte, to sketch and dance, and along the way, I managed to learn French and some Italian, too. But no Greek or Latin."

"I suppose French and Italian are much more useful in Society."

"Hardly, when we were at war with France for so long. I have rarely had occasion to practice either one," said Hetty tartly before remembering herself. She smiled and apologized for her unseemly outburst.

Jared watched the way her eyes lit up and wanted to tell her she could have all the outbursts she wanted if she would only continue to smile like that.

"You don't have to apologize to me, Hetty. But now that there's peace, do you think you will travel to France and Italy?"

"Oh, I don't know. My brother and his friend made their Grand Tour ten years ago—a short tour, of course. They were not all that impressed. And a woman traveling alone is rather awkward."

"I could go with you," he offered, gazing at her with such innocence she could not imagine he was being lewd.

"How kind of you to offer," said Hetty.

"Well, I always wanted to see France. There are lots of French people still living in New Orleans. I learned a little of their lingo."

Hetty had been about to correct his usage of slang in the presence of a lady, but Jared's next words, spoken so earnestly, robbed her of the ability to protest.

"Aimez, aimez, tout le reste n'est rien. It means . . ."

"Love, love, everything else is as nothing. That is from La Fontaine, isn't it?" said Hetty.

"So you do speak French, and very well," said Jared, raising his glass in salute.

Blushing, Hetty hurriedly finished her meal and led the way back to their schoolroom.

Several days later, Jared climbed out of his oversized bed and stretched, happily noting there was no stiffness to his movements as in the previous days. Hetty had been as good as her word in quickly securing the new bed.

He dressed with care, tying his cravat with ease, accustomed as he was to fending for himself. He raked a comb through his dark hair, and frowned. It had been too long since he had seen a barber. He would have to ask Norton or Sanders about that.

Sitting to put on his shoes, he was startled by the opening of the door that led to his little-used dressing room.

"Who are you?" he asked the unfamiliar figure dressed from head to toe in black.

"Gibbons. Your valet, my lord. At your service." The man hurried forward and took the shoe from Jared's hands. He proceeded to slide it on his stunned master's foot, then rose.

Jared stood up and looked down at the pinch-faced man. Though he was only an inch or two taller than the servant, Jared outweighed the gaunt Gibbons by twenty pounds. The man trembled slightly, but he did not turn away.

"Who hired you?" Jared demanded.

"Mr. Norton, my lord. He said you were in need of

someone who could advise you on a suitable wardrobe for a gentleman of style and good taste."

"He did, did he?"

"Yes, my lord. And if I may be permitted to say so, my lord, he was correct in his assessment. This coat will never do. And your linens!" The valet raised his hands in mock horror, then reached up and pulled Jared's cravat free.

Jared grabbed the man's wrists, saying slowly, "Let's get one thing straight, Gibbons. Norton may be right about the advice, but I'm not a dilettante when it comes to getting dressed. You can help me when I ask you, *if* I ask you. Otherwise, leave me alone."

"Of course, my lord, if that is what you wish," said the valet, his face crushed.

Jared groaned. "All right, all right. You can help with my demmed cravats. But that is all, and I don't want any of those fancy, can't-turn-my-head types."

"But perhaps I could trim your hair for you?" asked the skinny servant eagerly.

"Yes, yes. But no fussing over me. I am not a child!"

"Of course not, milord! If you would just have a seat, I will tend to the matter of your hair immediately."

Jared complied and watched in amazement as the efficient valet produced towels, scissors, and a hand mirror. He regarded his new man with growing respect as the servant clipped and trimmed, turning Jared's unruly curls into a perfect shape *à la Brutus*.

"There! I hope you are pleased, my lord."

"Very much so, Gibbons. Thank you."

The valet beamed and replied, "But that is my job, my lord. If you wish, I can shave you each day also." He produced a fresh cravat and tied it expertly in a complicated knot that still gave unrestricted movement.

"We shall see," said Jared, grunting with satisfaction as he studied the effect in the mirror. How easy it would be to sink into the habitual idleness for which the dandies of the *ton* were infamous. Still, he could see the advantage of having a talented valet.

"Gibbons, perhaps you could make up a list for me to take to the tailor," he said, turning to leave.

"Gladly, my lord, but I will contact the tailor and have him attend you here."

"As you wish," said Jared. He paused at the door, watching as the valet moved about, tidying the room, and singing quietly under his breath.

Jared listened in appreciation when he recognized the dirty little ditty as one the sailors had sung during the crossing to England. Perhaps there was more to the fusspot valet than first met the eye.

Descending the stairs, he met Hetty, who smilingly studied his elaborate cravat and shorn hair for a moment before saying, "I see you have met your new valet."

Jared gave her a crooked grin and nodded. "Is it so obvious?" he asked, forgetting for a moment his assumed role. He quickly added, "I reckon I look like a real gentleman now."

"Quite," said Hetty, taking the arm he offered.

When he had seated her in the chair beside his at

the breakfast table, she said, "We are going on an outing today."

"Outing? You mean we don't have to shut ourselves up in that little room all day long?"

She nodded.

"Wahoo!" he bellowed.

"Jared! Not so loud!" she admonished.

He leaned close to her ear and whispered, "Wahoo."

Hetty busied herself spreading jam on her toast, a thing she seldom did, and said sensibly, "I think we both need to get away from the house for the day. The weather is unseasonably warm, and I thought we would go for a drive in the country."

"Do I have a carriage?" asked Jared.

"Of course," said Hetty. "But if you don't drive, I would he happy to take the ribbons. I am quite accustomed to driving myself."

"That's not . . . very well. I kin drive a might, but I'm not much used t' city drivin'."

"Then it's settled. I have had Cook pack a basket for us." She consulted the gold watch hanging on a pendant around her neck. "The carriage should be outside by now. I'll just fetch my cloak. You should bring a coat. It may be chilly while we are driving."

Hetty had her hands full driving the light gig through the city streets. Though the *beau monde* still slept, the route was cluttered with vendors and carts. When they reached the open road, she let the restive cattle have their heads, and they bowled through the wintry countryside.

She turned off the main thoroughfare and followed a small track until they reached a meadow. Here, they abandoned the horses and walked across the field to a small stream. The sun shone brightly, warming their backs as they spread a blanket and sat down.

"Are you hungry?" asked Hetty.

"No, not right now," said Jared, lying back and letting the sunlight bathe him from head to toe.

Hetty removed her bonnet and lifted her face to the warmth, shutting her eyes and smiling slightly. Never would she have guessed she could be so at ease with a man. When she had come to London for her first Season, her father's warnings had filled her ears, transforming her into a suspicious, gauche dinner partner. Dancing had been impossible; she became all feet and arms.

He only wants your money, that voice would whisper in her ear, keeping time with the music better than she did. *He could not possibly care for you. You are too plain, too drab,* it said.

She had grown up since then, but having shut herself off from Society, she had never had a chance to prove her maturity, her sophistication. For several years, she daydreamed about going back to a ball and captivating the men with her grace, but that old voice still whispered in her ear, mocking her.

Now, however, with this rustic, this man of simple tastes . . . Hetty sat up and fumbled with the strings of her reticule before pulling out a volume of poetry.

Jared rolled onto his stomach and groaned. "Not more lessons, Hetty! It's too pretty to waste the day with lessons."

Hetty laughed, at ease again. Whatever might come of this alliance between them, she enjoyed his company. He made her feel confident . . . almost pretty.

"Just some poetry, Jared, and this time I will read to you. You must know the latest poets. When you go to routs and balls, everyone will have read Byron, or they will say they have."

"Who?"

"Lord Byron. Now listen to the rhythm, the words."

The Sea

> There is a pleasure in the pathless woods,
> There is a rapture on the lonely shore,
> There is society where none intrudes
> By the deep sea, and music in its roar;
> I love not man the less, but nature more,
> From these. . . .

"Is that supposed to make sense?" interrupted Jared, playing his part with genuine pleasure now. " 'Cause it doesn't. More like a lot of nonsense, if you ask me."

"How can you say so?" asked Hetty. "The poem is so powerful!"

"Perhaps to you, but who cares about the sea? Now, if you had read something by your Mr. Shakespeare or Mr. Donne . . ."

Hetty, displeased that he should deride her favorite romantic, Lord Byron, said tartly, "Such as?"

"Well now, let me think. I can't remember the name, but it goes something like this:

I wonder, by my troth, what thou and I
Did till we loved? were we not weaned till then,
But sucked on country pleasures, childishly?

Hetty's eyes grew misty as she listened to the beauty of the words, quoted in Jared's strong, even voice, with his very best pronunciation.

He continued through each stanza, finishing with,

If our two loves be one, or thou and I
Love so alike that none do slacken, none can die.

Hetty gulped a breath of fresh air as if she had been so spellbound, she had forgone breathing.

"Very good," she said hoarsely, trying to give the praise her best schoolmistress's voice, but failing, she was so moved. Smiling self-consciously, she added, "And that was by?"

"John Donne. Now I remember. It's called 'The Good Morrow,' " said Jared, his own exuberance subdued after he watched Hetty be carried away by the rendition.

He couldn't tell her it was the only one he knew by heart, and then only because it had been his mother's favorite. He had memorized it as a boy to get back in her good graces after some mischief. For some reason, he cared fervently that Hetty should think him an intelligent man, a man of some learning.

Breaking the spell, Jared said, "Let's see what Cook has sent."

The remainder of the morning was spent in companionable conversation. When Hetty asked Jared about his life in America, he told her of the time spent homesteading the unsettled wilderness rather than regaling her with tales of his gambling expertise in New Orleans. Though he carefully avoided examining his motives, he acknowledged that in the short time he had known her, he wanted this very proper English spinster to think the best of him.

"It is getting late, Jared. We should start back." Hetty stretched her muscles and sat up straight. Jared, who had been lying on his back, rose and pulled her effortlessly to her feet. His hands in hers, she remained a willing captive until they remembered themselves, dropped their hands, and resumed their prescribed roles.

"We should be going," she said again.

Jared was reluctant to have their idyllic day come to a close. Thinking quickly, he asked, "What type of dancing do they do over here?"

"Oh, there are all sorts. Many, like the quadrille, take four couples to make up a set," said Hetty, bending down for the blanket and starting to fold it. Jared took one end from her, stepped back, and bowed. Walking toward her in measured steps, he brought his two corners up to meet hers. Laughing, Hetty gave a half curtsy as they turned the cloth, separated, and met again in a type of minuet.

"Is that what they do?" asked Jared.

"Not precisely," said Hetty. "But we can hardly dance a quadrille with just the two of us."

"What about that waltz I heard about? Doesn't that take two?"

Hetty frowned, her suspicions roused. How had he heard of the scandalous dance?

"Maybe you don't know how," he challenged, his gaze wide and innocent.

"Of course I do," said Hetty. "I have performed it numerous times." That much was true. The dancing master she had hired for Margaret had insisted on teaching the steps to Hetty so she could model it for her pupil.

Humming an off-key tune, three slow beats to the measure, Hetty showed Jared how to hold her and placed her hand on his shoulder.

"One, two, three, one, two, three," she sang, closing her eyes and trying to remember that this was not a ballroom and she was not nineteen years old anymore.

Jared stopped after a few agonizing minutes, looking down at her with a frown. "Are you enjoying this?" he asked.

"I am a bit awkward at it. I haven't danced very much," she confessed, the old humiliation carrying her relentlessly back through the years, wiping away all the self-confidence she had imagined she now possessed.

"You must relax," he advised, placing her hand on his shoulder before taking her in a scandalously close embrace.

"Just to guide you," he said gruffly, excruciatingly aware of her fragrance, a whisper of lavender.

Humming in deep resonant tones, in perfect pitch, Jared guided Hetty through the steps of the waltz, their speed increasing as they grew accustomed to the rhythm of the music. Laughing at the sheer freedom from care, they moved as one. His voice rising in a closing crescendo, Jared gave Hetty a final twirl and lost his footing on the grass. He fell on his backside, his feet tangled in Hetty's skirts. She landed on top of him, suffering more from a fit of the giggles than any injury.

"Are you hurt?" he asked anxiously.

"No!" she managed before dissolving into laughter again.

It was contagious, and Jared joined in, wrapping his arms around her as she rested her head on his chest, gasping for air. She rolled onto the grass, still laughing, and Jared followed, leaning over her and gazing down at her smiling face.

Her giggles stopped. Jared's smile faded. His eyes sought her lips. Her breathing stilled as she waited.

"We should be going," he said softly.

She couldn't respond.

"Come along," he said, climbing to his feet and offering her a hand to help her rise. She looked at it before turning away and rising without assistance.

Quickly, they gathered the basket and the neatly folded blanket and returned to the carriage.

Five

What ecstasies her bosom fire!
How her eyes languish with desire!
How blest, how happy should I be,
Were that fond glance bestow'd on me!
                                        —*John Gay*

"I'll take the ribbons," said Jared, placing his hands around Hetty's waist and lifting her easily into the carriage. He placed the basket under the seat and climbed up by her side.

"Are you sure you wish to drive, Jared? These horses are quite a handful." Hetty grinned when he rolled his blue eyes to the heavens. "Very well, but if you wish, I can take over when we reach the city. It can be rather tricky handling a pair in traffic," said Hetty.

Jared turned the carriage and picked up the whip, touching the horses' flanks lightly and sending them along the narrow track at an alarming pace.

"Jared!" called Hetty, her voice lost behind them as they bowled along, their speed increasing sharply when they attained the main road.

Another snap of the whip, and the horses fairly flew down the road, not slowing until the buildings on each side became more numerous.

"Do you want to take over?" asked Jared, slowing enough to turn and look at her.

"You *are* a rogue," she laughed, holding on with one hand while extending her arm to point the way home with the other.

Hetty had no trouble falling asleep that night, and if her dreams were of ballrooms and a certain tall gentleman, she managed to ignore the implications until she awoke.

Even in the early morning light, she told herself she had imagined the tension, the desire in his eyes. She mounted her old mare, Daisy, and cantered away from the house, little troubled by her dreams.

"After all," she said, conversing with herself as she rode through the empty park, "I have been ignoring my daydreams of knights in shining armor for years. There is no reason to read anything into the dreams I have while I sleep. It's no mystery why the hero of those dreams closely resembles the marquess. He is an incredibly handsome, charming, virile man."

Did I really say virile? she thought.

Jared, for some inexplicable reason, woke early, his sleep restless and unfulfilling. Rising, he wandered downstairs in search of a little something to tide him over until breakfast. His arrival in the kitchen so alarmed the cook, she let the toast burn.

"I assure you, I like it very brown," he assured her, his comment causing her to burst into tears.

"Oh, milord, you are too kind!" she exclaimed, smiling and crying simultaneously while he patted her plump shoulder.

"I am only sorry I startled you. I often went foraging in the kitchen when I was at home. I didn't realize it would be considered strange here," he said, picking up a piece of blackened bread and nibbling at it gingerly.

The cook took it away from him, clucking like a hen. "We can't have you eating this rubbish, milord. Here's a bit of apple tart for you, just t' take the edge off yer appetite. I'll have the rest ready in a trice."

"Thank you, Mrs. . . . ?"

"Anderson," she said, bobbing a curtsy.

"Thank you, Mrs. Anderson. I have been meaning to come and tell you how very much I like your cooking, especially that lamb dish with the turnips."

"The harrico of mutton. Thank you, milord. That 'uns Mr. Anderson's favorite, too," said the cook, beaming with pleasure.

"Does Mr. Anderson work here also?"

" 'E helps in th' garden, thank you, milord."

"Well, I will let you return to your work, Mrs. Anderson. Thank you for taking such good care of us here."

"Yer welcome, milord," she said, bobbing another curtsy.

Jared wandered back up the stairs, his hunger appeased for the moment. When he arrived in the front hall, he met Hetty as she entered from her morning ride.

"Good morning, my lord."

"Good morning, Miss Thompson," he replied, admiring the pink of her cheeks and the sparkle in her eyes. "Where have you been?"

"Out riding," she said, laying her gloves on the table in the hall and removing her hat, a rakish affair with a curling plume. Checking her hair in the mirror, she smiled over her shoulder at his reflection. "I would have asked you to accompany me, but I knew Mr. Norton wouldn't want you parading around the park until we are ready to spring you on the world."

"What the devil? I really don't care what Mr. Norton wants."

"Are you so very bored?" she asked sympathetically.

"Very," he snapped. "I'm almost ready to bolt."

Sanders shuffled into the hall and drew himself up to his full height, announcing loudly, "Breakfast, my lord."

"I will be down in a few minutes," she said, tripping lightly up the stairs to change.

When she entered the dining room a few minutes later, Jared rose and seated her, his behavior and manners exactly as they should be.

"You are certainly a quick study, Jared," said Hetty, selecting some stewed plums from the offerings.

They had been working less than a fortnight and already the new marquess's speech had improved remarkably. He was certainly ready for the outing she had planned.

"Why, thank you, Hetty," he said slowly and clearly, a smile seeking her approval. "You look very pretty in that gown. It reminds me of those jonquils we were talking about."

"Thank you," she said, her eyes lighting with pleasure.

Sanders entered with a fresh pot of tea and served his mistress. Their conversation became innocuous as they finished their meal.

Then Hetty sat back and grinned at him, looking like the cat that drank the cream. As if speaking to a child, she said, "I have a surprise for you today, Jared. We are going to go to the museum."

"What kind of museum?" he asked, masking his amusement with an ingenuous smile and wide eyes.

"It is the Royal Academy of Arts. There are many fine works of art—painting, sculptures, and so on. We will also see the famous Elgin Marbles, which were brought back from Greece."

"And I'm supposed to be interested in all this, my being a marquess and all?"

"But you will be, Jared. There are some remarkable works there. And then, if you enjoy landscape paintings, there are Constables and Turners. There are a number by Gainsborough, who was very famous for his portraits. Some of the paintings are twice as tall as you are! It is most extraordinary."

"Then what are we waiting for?" he asked, taking her hand in his and pulling her toward the door.

"Wait, Jared!" she laughed. "First, you have your appointment with the tailor. He should be here any moment."

"Ugh! I dislike being poked and prodded."

"But you want to look your best."

"Oh, very well. But will you help?" When she looked startled, he said, "I mean to select my clothes."

"I think Gibbons is more suitable for that, Jared," said Hetty.

"But what if he likes bright colors and stripes that aren't at all appropriate for the *ton?*"

She sighed and said, "Oh, very well. First, have him measure you. Then we will speak to the tailor together."

When the tailor had finished scribbling Jared's measurements, Gibbons was sent for Hetty, who entered reluctantly. She felt the awkwardness of her position, neither servant nor a close relation. The tailor studied her with surreptitious curiosity, but he said nothing.

"What could I possibly want with all these coats, Gibbons? Surely three would be enough," said Jared, frowning at the list his valet had made for the tailor.

"Certainly not, sir," said the valet, emphasizing slightly the "sir."

They had agreed any outsiders visiting the house should be given the impression that its occupant was a plain mister. Hetty wished they had thought to pretend she was Jared's wife or sister to lend her respectability.

"And what does madam think?" asked Gibbons, deferring to her opinion.

Hetty thought the tailor looked on her with dawning respect.

"Gibbons is correct, my dear," she said, smiling sweetly at Jared's shocked reaction. "If you are to go about in Society, you will have to be well dressed. That means having many more coats than you needed in the Colonies."

Jared handed the tailor the note, saying, "If that's what th' little woman thinks, it's good enough for me!"

Gibbons closed the door as he left Jared's sitting room to escort the tailor outside. Jared took one look at Hetty and roared with laughter. Hetty's clutched her sides, rocking back and forth, overcome with silent giggles.

Wiping tears from her eyes, she said, "I thought I would burst when I called you 'my dear'! The look on your face!"

"You should have had a mirror when I called you the little woman!" he exclaimed.

Their laughter finally subsided to an occasional giggle. Hetty suddenly realized where she was—alone with the handsome marquess. That old, terrible shyness washed over her, and she dropped her eyes to her lap.

Rising, she said, "I must send for the carriage and fetch my hat and cloak."

Puzzled by the sudden change in her demeanor, Jared teased, "I'll be down in a minute, Mrs. Winter."

Hetty gave him a nervous smile and closed the door. They met at the top of the stairs a few moments later. All her reserve had faded, and Hetty whispered, "Are you ready, husband?"

"If you are, Mrs. Winter," he laughed.

Watching the couple descend the stairs, Sanders smiled benignly on them from his post near the door. Jared caught the old man's eye and nodded to him. While Hetty was checking her hat in the hall mirror, he strolled over to Sanders, who rose to meet him. With a gentle hand, Jared pushed the servant back into his chair.

"I *will* take care of her," he said quietly.

"I trust you will, my lord," said the servant, his sharp eyes never wavering. "My lady comes from a very old and distinguished family. There is more to her than you might think, my lord."

"I'm ready," announced Hetty, who was dressed in a black cloak and had topped her soft brown curls with a veiled bonnet.

Jared accepted his own cloak from the footman. Favoring Hetty with an intimate smile, he offered her his arm. She might look like a crow in mourning, but he knew what lay beneath the surface, and he planned to make the most of this day.

While they were strolling through the galleries of the Royal Academy, Hetty maintained a steady flow of information, her eyes fixed on the works of art that lined the walls. Jared spared a moment for each painting or work of sculpture, made a comment, and then returned to his study of Hetty.

How, he wondered, had she ever escaped matrimony? She was well educated, but not to the point of being a bluestocking. She was a wonderful conversationalist, able to sustain discourse on many subjects, ranging from art and literature to the political and social concerns of the day. Most of all, she was quite pretty, much more so than he had thought upon first meeting her.

"Why are you wearing that hideous veil?" he asked suddenly, interrupting her observations on some painter's masterpiece.

"What?" she asked, startled.

"That veil. I realize we have not had the opportunity to go about very much, but you have not worn it before."

"We have not gone to such a public place before, my lord," she whispered.

"What did you call our picnic?" he asked, his voice at normal volume.

"A country outing. It is not the same thing," said Hetty, pulling him to one side of the empty room. "It was unlikely we would meet anyone in the country."

He flipped up her veil so he could see her face better, then held her arms at her sides so she could not restore it. "Who are you trying to protect, Hetty, you or me?"

"Jared, please. Neither of us would benefit by being recognized in this place." Her eyes begged him to release her, and he did. Hetty covered her face, all the while darting furtive glances around the near-empty room.

"Are you ready to go home?" she asked.

"No, no. By all means continue my education."

"Very well. I want to show you these two over here. You see how Constable and Turner . . . Jared, where are you taking me?"

"I want your opinion of this one, Hetty," he said, his eyes twinkling with mischief. "I think it is spectacular: the lines, the colors, the models."

"Jared, you are incorrigible!" Hetty was unable to stifle a giggle.

Jared gazed at the large painting, which depicted a soldier on horseback trying to hold on to two nude females. Hetty shook her head and walked away. Jared fell into step by her side, his hand taking hers and placing it on his arm, covering it possessively.

He leaned close to her veiled ear and whispered, "I know I am a gambler, but even if I weren't, I would wager there is, at this very moment, the most enchanting blush staining your cheeks, Miss Thompson."

"Incorrigible!" she returned, her voice quivering with suppressed laughter. "Now this one . . ."

"How can you say Constable's paintings are flat?" demanded Hetty as they entered the house again late in the afternoon.

"Well, ma'am," said Jared, cognizant of the servants lingering in the front hall, "I reckon they have a few animals and people in them, but the land looks dead. I mean, when was the last time you looked out across a pasture and saw anything so still? No, give me Raphael any day!"

"You simply like all those ladies!" She giggled as

she pulled off her hat and veil and handed them to the butler.

Sanders forgot himself so much that he allowed them to fall to the floor.

"Beg pardon, miss," he said, taking hold of the sideboard which held the daily mail to bend over. By this time, Jared had retrieved the headgear and handed it to the aging butler.

Hetty patted the old man's arm, causing him to sway in alarm. "Think nothing of it," she said, sweeping past him and into the salon. "We are famished, Sanders. Would you ask Cook to make up a tea tray?"

"Certainly, miss. Right away." Sanders spared a brief nod for Jared, who winked at him.

Jared entered the salon, his presence filling the room.

"I sure enjoyed our day," he said quietly, wishing for the hundredth time he could drop his act completely and be himself. But Hetty would never forgive him for duping her.

"It was wonderful, wasn't it? I don't know when I have enjoyed a visit to the museum quite as much. Thank you, Jared."

"I should be thankin' you, Hetty. I learned a lot about art today," he said, feeling more foolish with every word.

"Nonsense! You seem to have an innate appreciation for the arts. Have you ever done any painting yourself?"

"Just a wall or two." He ducked his head and peered up at her with a boyish grin.

"You are impossible," she said, laughing.

"What about you?" he asked. "Do you have a studio hidden someplace?"

She blushed and shook her head. "I am not very talented with my hands, except . . . but no, in answer to your question, I do not paint."

Her obvious reticence intrigued him, and he asked, "But there is something you do, isn't there? Ah, I can tell by the blush you have some hidden talent. What is it? Let me guess!" He paced the length of the room and back again before coming to stand in front of her. "I know it isn't singing," he said.

"Beast," she laughed.

Snapping his fingers, he said, "I have it! You're a dancer!"

"Only in the ballroom, my lord," laughed Hetty.

"Or on picnics," he murmured, raising one brow before resuming his pensive stroll. Stopping again, he said, "Sculptor? No? Then perhaps you do sing; only humming is beyond your ability."

"Definitely not, although I enjoy the activity. My brother always says my voice sounds as if I am strangling the cat."

"Kind brother," observed Jared. Snapping his fingers again, he said, "You play the harp? The pianoforte?"

"Only passably," said Hetty, giggling at his absurdity.

"Then you must tell me. I am all out of guesses."

"I play the lyre. It is an ancient instrument, rather like a small harp. I make them, too, but that is a different sort of pleasure. I enjoy creating something out of nothing."

Jared sat on the sofa by her side, saying, "You make them?"

Hetty nodded. "I have the wood cut to the basic shape, then I put them together, add the strings, and so on."

"I am in awe," he said. "I never dreamed you were so talented."

"It is hardly a great talent, Jared, especially when I sing along. I still sound like I'm strangling the cat."

"Do you have one here?"

"Well, yes, but . . ."

Jared crossed the room and tugged the bellpull. Sanders appeared immediately.

"Be so good as to have Miss Thompson's maid fetch her lyre to the parlor."

The butler looked past him to Hetty for confirmation, then nodded and toddled away.

"Jared, I warn you, my playing is only passable."

"But you make them," he said again, clearly impressed.

Moments later, Hetty was turning pink as she plucked the tune of "Barbra Allen." Jared hummed along at first, then joined in singing the words in a clear baritone while Hetty switched to playing chords.

When they finished, they shared a contented sigh.

"You have a lovely voice," she said.

"And you have the fingers of an angel!" he vowed.

Laughing, Hetty put down the instrument. "I shall have to warn all the innocent young ladies what a flatterer you are. They won't be safe around you."

"What innocent young ladies?"

"The ones who will positively swoon when they

learn the new Marquess Winter, along with his fortune, has arrived in London in need of a wife," said Hetty, dropping her gaze and wondering suddenly why her lighthearted mood had fled, leaving in its wake a black cloud to float over her.

"Didn't know I was in need of a wife," he said lightly.

"But you must wed, Jared. Winterhurst needs an heir," she said, her voice hollow. Smiling with false gaiety, she added, "And the young ladies of London will simply fall at your feet!"

"What makes you think I care about them?" he asked softly, a frown erasing his ready smile.

Hetty's breath caught in her dry throat. Their eyes met, then retreated. Jared covered her hand with his.

"Hetty, I . . ."

The door opened. Jared pulled his hand away, and Sanders entered, followed by a footman straining under the weight of a full tray.

Silence reigned in the presence of the servants. When they had gone, Hetty busied herself pouring the tea while Jared thoughtfully downed a biscuit. By the time they had both been served, the moment of truth had passed, and they fell to making light conversation in the manner Hetty had taught Jared.

"You know, Hetty, when I first agreed to come to England, Mr. Norton kept going on about a maiden speech. Do you know what he was talking about? At first, I thought he meant how I talked to women, but I don't think that was it."

Hetty's eyes widened, and she said, "Of course! I

should have thought of that before. Your first speech to the House of Lords."

"The House of Lords? No, he can't have meant that. I have no political aspirations!"

Hetty studied him, frowning. "Sometimes, Jared, you surprise me with your vocabulary."

"I did read sometimes," he hedged. "Just because I don't always say the words proper like doesn't mean I don't understand them."

"Certainly not. I meant no offense." Hetty touched the sleeve of his coat, then quickly withdrew her hand. The gesture propelled them back to their previous uncomfortable silence.

After several moments, Hetty ventured, "Jared, I . . ."

Sanders entered the salon again. His shadow, the footman, hurried past him to pick up the depleted tray and carry it away.

"Will there be anything else, miss?"

"No, Sanders, that is all." Hetty rose. Giving Jared a sad smile, she said, "I must go and change. I believe the hem of my gown is damp. Won't you excuse me?"

"Certainly," he replied gruffly, watching her departure before finishing with, "my dear."

Jared received Hetty's note with a frown. It was craven of her to refuse to come down to dinner. He didn't believe for a minute she was ill. She simply meant to avoid him. Their camaraderie of the day had become uncomfortable for her, and she had withdrawn into her timid shell.

"I ought to go in there and drag her to the table," he muttered, forgetting for a moment that Sanders was serving him and might take exception to his words. Taking another sip of his wine, Jared glared at the butler.

"Don't worry, I won't disturb her."

In a foul mood by the time he had finished the bottle of red wine, Jared returned to his room, glowered at Gibbons, and poured a glass of whiskey from the decanter on his escritoire.

"Women!" he said, raising the glass in a mock toast before downing its contents in one gulp.

He settled into one of the chairs beside the fire—the one, he recalled, where he had been sitting that first night when Hetty had helped him dislodge his boot. He grinned at the memory. She hadn't acted the shy miss then.

"Have you ever been married, Gibbons?" asked Jared.

The valet paused in his task of turning down the bed. "No, my lord. Having gone to sea at the age of ten, I never had the opportunity when I was of an age."

"Lucky man. What made you leave the sea?"

"I was a small boy for my age. They called me 'Tiny' because I had reached my twentieth birthday and barely stood level to the captain's shoulder. Suddenly, I began to grow, and that's when the trouble started. I kept hitting my head all the time, my voice changed, and I was terribly clumsy. But the worst part was I grew seasick at the first whitecap. I couldn't do my duty, and I was miserable about it."

"What happened?"

"My captain told me I would have to leave the navy. I was that sad, my lord. I was at Trafalgar when Lord Nelson defeated the entire French Navy! I had grown to manhood on a ship, and I planned to grow old in the service of his Majesty's navy. It nearly broke my heart, it did."

"I'm sorry, Gibbons," said Jared, reflecting that he wasn't the only one whose life had not gone according to plan. Who would have thought he would become an English lord?

"I've gotten used to it, my lord."

"But how did you go from cabin boy to valet?"

"My captain's brother needed a man and was willing to train me if I was willing to work for the privilege. I took him up on the offer, and the rest, as they say, is history."

"I, for one, am glad you did, Gibbons. You're a credit to your profession."

"Thank you, my lord." The valet straightened his stooped shoulders in pride.

"Do you play piquet?" asked Jared.

"A passable game, my lord."

"Then pour each of us a drink and join me," said Jared, shuffling a deck of cards.

"If you insist, my lord."

The next morning, Hetty dressed in her most severe gown, a dark brown sarcenet with long sleeves and a high neckline. She avoided the breakfast room, going straight to the study and setting out several books to test Jared's mathematics skills.

An evening spent in contemplation had convinced her that she had allowed the student-teacher relationship to deteriorate so much that disaster was imminent. No good could come of the easy camaraderie she had allowed between them. It was not as if the Marquess of Winter would ever choose to wed an aging spinster who had set herself up as a private tutor.

She, at least, knew the ways of Society. Jared did not. After he had made his bow, if he were to greet her in public with untoward warmth, it would signal her ruin. Her family would be furious, and rightly so. Because they loved her, they condoned her rather eccentric behavior. They did not deserve to have their name dragged in the mud.

When Jared entered, she remained behind the massive desk and bestowed a tight smile on her pupil.

"Good morning, Jared."

"Good morning, Hetty. Did you sleep well?"

"Yes, thank you."

"I was sorry your headache kept you in bed. I missed you at dinner. I hope you're better."

"Much, thank you. But, Jared, you should not inquire how I slept. It isn't proper."

"All right, I'll try to remember. No sleep, no beds when talking to ladies. Am I supposed to assume ladies simply don't sleep in beds? Because I assure you, the ladies I know do so. Well, sometimes they sleep," he added outrageously.

"Jared!"

He grinned, but she wouldn't relent, keeping her mask of disapproval firmly in place.

He expelled a disgruntled sigh, saying in a childish pitch, "Yes, miss. Whatever you say, miss."

Hetty ignored him, saying, "Good. Now today I thought we would work on your ciphering skills. I have set out several types of problems here on the desk which you will endeavor to solve while I attend to some household matters," she added, slipping away to the far side of the desk as he moved behind it. "I will leave you to your work."

Jared sat down and quickly finished the problems. He turned and stared into the rain-soaked garden. A ray of sunshine was breaking through the clouds. He wondered idly if the cheery sunbeam lightened his mood or merely accented the gloom he had felt when Hetty left the room.

Rising, he strode to the door, threw it open, and bellowed, "Miss Thompson!" *Devil take the servants!* He shouted, "Hetty! Hetty!"

"Jared! What is it?" she demanded, hurrying into view.

"I've finished, miss," he said, smiling proudly.

She studied his blue eyes for the telltale twinkle. Seeing none, her nose rose several inches and she swept past him, quickly putting the desk between them again. Still suspicious, she began to check his work, looking up from time to time to give him a frowning nod.

Each problem was perfectly solved, neatly written. She lifted her head to congratulate him, but Jared had taken advantage of her concentration and slipped behind the desk. Leaning over her, his hands touched the back of her chair. The room, damp and cool only moments before, became tropical, and Hetty blushed a fiery red. Jared's hands moved slowly up her arms to her shoulders.

She turned to protest, but found herself suddenly bereft of speech as his lips brushed hers. Shivering, she managed only a whimper before his lips returned, slowly moving against hers as his hands continued to torture her arms, teasing her with an ephemeral embrace.

"Good morning!" called Tobias Norton loudly.

"Good morning, Norton." Jared gave the briefest of nods as he moved quickly away from Hetty. In perfectly clipped accents, he added coldly, "I would have thought Sanders would announce you. I think that is how things are done here."

Hetty's eyes widened. Surely his accent was not that good before.

"I'm sorry, my lord. I didn't realize how busy you were. How are the lessons going?" asked the solicitor.

"Very well, I think. I daresay I shall soon be ready to acquit myself quite admirably in Parliament. I assume you have arranged for me to make that maiden speech you were so keen on."

"Yes, yes, of course, my lord. Miss Thompson, what do you say? Is his lordship ready to make his bow in Society?"

Hetty's generous breasts rose and fell quickly as she looked from one to the other. He had been making game of her all this time. Of course his mathematics problems were correct. He was no country bumpkin!

Her breathing became irregular. She stifled a gasp, and her eyes opened wide with horror. Jared grinned at her sheepishly.

"Oh!" she said, edging toward the door. "Yes, Mr. Norton. Our lessons have gone so well, I find there is no longer any need for my services. Good-bye!"

With that, Hetty fled, speeding up the stairs and throwing open her door. To her startled maid, she called, "Molly, pack my things! We are going home!" She turned the key in the lock and began to open drawers.

Hearing the commotion abovestairs, Jared growled a curse and hurried past the startled solicitor.

"Hetty! Open this door!" he demanded, trying the knob and finding it was locked.

"Miss! What shall we do? He's gone mad!" exclaimed the frightened maid.

"Ignore him and pack!" Hetty ordered.

"Hetty! I warn you! Open this blasted door!"

"Go away!" she shouted.

"The hell I will!"

Jared's kick splintered the hinges, sending the door crashing into the room, accompanied by Hetty's screamed protest. The valiant maid stepped between her mistress and the madman only to be firmly set to one side.

Giving Hetty a shake, Jared glared at her and demanded, "Now! Does that satisfy you that I'm still in need of your tutelage?"

Molly crumpled to the floor. Hetty pushed past Jared, kneeling beside her servant and shooting dagger glances up at him.

"Now look what you've done!" she declared.

"Exactly!" he returned, glowering at her and the maid.

"You are an uncivilized beast!"

"Undoubtedly!" said Jared, relaxing a little.

"Have you no idea how to behave?" she asked, a tiny glimmer softening the anger in her eyes.

"None!" he said, taking a step toward her.

One raised, slim hand held him at bay.

"Hand me the smelling salts on the dressing table," she commanded. As she waved them under Molly's nose, the maid groaned.

Hetty glanced up at Jared and said, "Later we will discuss the proper way for a gentleman to enter a room, my lord."

"With pleasure, Miss Thompson. With pleasure."

Six

Thou'll break my heart, thou bonnie bird
That sings upon the bough;
Thou minds me o' the happy days
When my fause Luve was true.
*   —Robert Burns*

Dinner that evening was made easier for both Jared and Hetty by the presence of Tobias Norton, which allowed each a certain quantity of distraction. The need to pay attention at the conscious level prevented them from dwelling on the new dilemma they faced.

Conversation centered around politics as Hetty and the solicitor tried to inform Jared about the various political parties and stances. Jared, for his part, listened with outward attentiveness, but he found it difficult to treat the topic with the sobriety he detected in both Hetty and Norton.

"The Prince Regent, some believe, will side with the Whigs when the old king dies," said Norton in answer to Jared's question.

"And if he changes his mind?"

"He wouldn't!" exclaimed the solicitor nervously, as if this particular idea had not occurred to him.

Hetty shook her head, saying sensibly, "If he were to side with the whigs, he would alienate almost every thinking member of Parliament. The Whigs believed he would oust the Tories when he became Regent, and he didn't. I don't see how he could change his mind now. After all this time, to make such an about-face would lose him the trust of both sides, I should think."

"Perhaps," said Jared, admiring her shrewd analysis and the way the candlelight shone in her eyes. Not wanting to dampen her enthusiasm, he continued playing the devil's advocate. "But surely when he is king, his own interests will change as well. What is good and convenient for the Prince Regent may be totally wrong for King George IV."

"He would not!" reiterated Norton, unable to relinquish his stance or his faith in the status quo.

"He might, I grant you," said Hetty judiciously.

"So do you still think I, the Marquess of Winter, should totally embrace the Tories? Would it not be more expedient, until I can form my own opinions on each issue, for me to avoid taking sides?"

Hetty smiled appreciatively and nodded. Norton, who was himself a staunch Tory, was slower to agree. But Jared didn't care. If Hetty approved, that was good enough for him.

Changing the subject to a more personal concern, Norton said, "I had a visit from your cousin today, my lord."

"Which one? The limp one or the brute?" asked Jared.

"Mr. Golightly," said Norton, turning to Hetty and inquiring, "Are you acquainted with Mr. Casper Golightly or his mother?"

"I believe I met Mrs. Golightly once," said Hetty, unwilling to admit she had often seen Mrs. Golightly. Her son, Casper, had made an offer for Hetty's hand during her fourth and last Season. Mrs. Golightly had discovered Hetty's portion was not the fortune her son had been led to believe and had intervened—not that Hetty would have accepted.

"Then you understand why I want Lord Winter to be completely transformed before meeting them. And then there is the other cousin."

"Who is that?" asked Hetty.

"Sylvester Perdue. I daresay you have not heard of him, Miss Thompson. He is on the fringe of Society. One never reads about his exploits in the social columns," said the solicitor.

"No money?" said Jared.

"The lack of funds is, I believe, the least of Mr. Perdue's problems," Norton replied.

"I have heard of Mr. Perdue, but I have never met him, of course," Hetty said.

"I am not surprised. He is in trade."

"And going into business makes him unacceptable to Society?"

"Indeed, Jared, money is not the only *entrée* to the *ton*. One's birth has a great deal to do with it. And your cousin, though he is acceptable in rank, has chosen to make himself unacceptable by questionable business dealings," said Hetty. "You see, one can have money, but to go out and earn it, especially in some-what shady circumstances, well, that is unacceptable."

If there had been any doubt Hetty was a member of the *ton,* or had been, her insight erased it from Jared's mind. She was born to mingle in the four hun-dred, as the *ton* was known.

"What has he done?" asked Jared.

Norton cleared his throat and said, "He has an in-terest in several houses of . . ." The solicitor blushed hotly and shook his head. "It is not a suitable topic to discuss in Miss Thompson's presence."

"He runs brothels." Hetty grinned wickedly. How wonderful it was to care nothing for her proper place in the world.

Jared threw back his head and laughed at the irony. Some might have called his house in New Orleans a brothel, since Angel had rented her apartment of rooms from him.

Norton frowned, still shaking his head. "It is ru-mored Mr. Perdue also owns shares in a shipping com-pany whose chief export is slaves."

Sobering, Jared said, "Well, well. I begin to dislike this cousin of mine."

"Anyway, Mr. Golightly, who is next in line, is ami-able enough and hardly likely to cause trouble by con-testing your right to the marquessate. But his mother and Mr. Perdue? That is another story entirely!" said Norton, rising and pacing the length of the room.

Hetty rose also, saying, "If you will excuse me, gen-tlemen, I don't think this concerns me."

"Nonsense! Of course it does," exclaimed Jared, wondering privately at his own vehemence.

"You can share it with me later, Jared, if you wish. For now, I will leave you to your port."

Sanders entered, setting out two glasses and several decanters. Norton returned to his chair and accepted a glass from Jared.

A thoughtful silence prevailed. Finally, Norton extracted a large handkerchief and wiped his brow twice. Then the nervous little solicitor proceeded to swirl the ruby liquid for several minutes before Jared lost patience.

"Out with it!" he barked.

Norton took a quick swallow, and squeaked, "Very well, my lord. I hate to play the prude, but you cannot continue to live here under these circumstances. It is quite obvious you have been gammoning Miss Thompson into thinking you were an ignorant provincial. Her eyes have now been opened, however, and it would be most improper . . ."

"The devil take you and your 'impropers,' Norton!" snapped Jared, rising and pacing the length of the table before returning to stand behind his chair, his strong hands gripping the back as he glared at the stubborn solicitor.

"Hetty—"

"Miss Thompson," said the solicitor firmly, "is from a fine family, a very powerful family."

"Hetty—Miss Thompson, that is—is in no danger from me. I promise you, word of a Winter, I will do nothing to harm her."

"Actions are not necessary, my lord, for it to spell ruin for Miss Thompson. The fact you have lived in the same house will suffice. If you were related, it would be different."

Jared's frown deepened. "Did you say she is from a powerful family?" The solicitor nodded, and Jared asked, "They can't be a very caring one. Have they not wondered where she is?"

"I'm sure I couldn't say, my lord. But with your entrance into the political arena—and therefore, Society—it would be safest for all concerned if Miss Thompson left. The situation, should it become known, would do neither of you any credit. As I said, her family . . ."

"I know, is powerful. Who are they?"

"I really couldn't say. My source of information, a former colleague, mentioned something about a duke-dom. I don't know how Miss Thompson is related, but I feel it is safe to say her family is extremely power-ful."

"You think she is royalty?" asked Jared doubtfully.

"I really don't know, my lord, but it would not do to cross them," said Norton.

"So they are more powerful than the Winters." Jared's jaw clenched with some undefined emotion.

"Yes, my lord, I believe so."

"Do you think I would turn craven because of that?" demanded Jared suddenly.

"No, my lord," said Norton quietly. "I perceive you would willingly face the demons of hell to defend the lady in question. However, in this instance, physical bravery is not required. Miss Thompson is in danger of being placed beyond the pale, of being irrevocably ruined by her role in this episode, her presence in your house."

Jared turned away, saying quietly, "And yet you hired her."

"Yes. I thought it best for you at the time, and I was under the impression, you will recall, that I would be bringing back a youth. Still, I would have done anything to see my mission succeed, and that is why I wanted her to remain. I am as much at fault as you, my lord, and I feel it keenly. But now things have changed, and shortly your presence in London will become common knowledge. People will call on you, invite you to attend balls and such."

"And Hetty? What will become of her?"

"She will return to her house, find other students, and take up her life as before, if she can," said Norton, using his handkerchief to blow his nose.

"But why does she do that—teach, I mean—if her family is so influential?" cried Jared, whirling to face the solicitor again.

"I don't know, my lord. Only Miss Thompson could tell you that. I only know from this informant that even before she came here, her activities had caused many to avoid her. Not only was she a teacher, but she lived on her own, away from the protection of her family. For an unmarried female to do that . . . well, it was rumored she was in the keeping of a man."

"Rubbish! Hetty would never do anything so dishonorable! She is good and honest, and . . ." Jared sat down again, his energy spent. After several moments, he growled, "If we were wed?"

Norton bowed his head, unable to meet Jared's

fierce gaze. "She would not accept it, my lord. Miss Thompson knows what marriage means in this Society. It is most often a business arrangement."

"And if I promised her it wasn't like that?"

"Do you think she would believe you? Even if she did, Miss Thompson would not wish it. She would want you to consider your position, your rank."

"Is that all any of you care about?" demanded Jared. He sank into the chair, his head bowed, and said bitterly, "You know what, Norton? I wish you had never come to New Orleans."

Hetty dressed with care the next morning before descending to the dining room. When she entered, Jared was before her, stirring his coffee, his demeanor distracted. His plate was untouched.

"Good morning, my lord." She went to the sideboard to serve herself with food she knew she wouldn't be able to eat.

"Hetty, we must talk," Jared said when she was seated. He favored her with a rueful smile, saying, "I must, anyway."

"Very well," she said, subdued by his suddenly intense manner.

"I have to apologize to you for my inexcusable behavior."

"I accept," she said, smiling at him, her brown eyes warm and kind.

"I don't deserve . . . what did you say?" he asked.

"I said I forgive you, Jared."

"But you haven't even asked why I tried to make a fool of you."

"Well, I prefer to think of it as a harmless joke, not an effort to ridicule me. But then again, I have always been too forgiving of the men in my life."

Jared grinned. "Lucky men." He frowned, adding, "What men are those?"

Hetty laughed again. "Oh, fathers, brothers, the usual assortment. With a brother like mine, I grew accustomed over the years to forgiving all sorts of tomfoolery."

"You're an exceptional woman, Miss Thompson," said Jared, smiling fondly at her. He took a deep breath and shook his head. "It won't do, however. I intend to make a clean sweep of it. I was a cad, and I feel the need to explain."

Hetty replaced her teacup on its saucer and folded her hands in her lap, waiting for him to begin.

His blue eyes were twinkling as he told her how insulted he had felt at first, how he had determined to pretend to be as stupid as she supposed him to be.

"But, Jared, I didn't think you were stupid because you came from the Colonies. I just couldn't believe any man would dare to do what you did—have me act as your valet! And you could barely put two words together."

"I was bowled over by your beauty," he said, only half teasing.

"Fustian! Now I know you are gammoning me. There I was with my hair falling about my shoulders, wearing a tattered old wrapper, and barefoot!"

The memory imposed a bemused smile on Jared's handsome face as he murmured, "Exactly, my dear."

Hetty blushed and said self-consciously, "I guessed soon enough, you know, that you were much better educated than you at first indicated. Where did you have your schooling? Did your father send you back here for school?"

Jared followed her lead, saying, "No, I went to school in Virginia for two years. I was so homesick. I hated it. Finally, I persuaded my father to allow me to return home. I was fourteen by then. He made me keep up my studies."

"What of your mother?" asked Hetty, relaxing now that the topic had changed.

"My mother was the daughter of a vicar. Her grandfather was Irish, and that made her unacceptable to the Winters. I hated my grandfather, the old marquess, and I never even met him. When I was a boy and heard my mother crying because she had robbed me of my inheritance, I vowed I would come here and murder him for disowning my parents."

"How terrible for you." Hetty placed her fingers over his.

Jared took her capable hand in his and gave it a gentle squeeze. Hetty leaned toward him, her cheeks coloring with anticipation.

"I've brought a fresh pot of tea, miss," said Sanders, entering the dining room unannounced.

Hetty snatched her hand back to her lap, saying airily, "Thank you, Sanders, but I am finished. Shall we work in the salon today, my lord?" she added as she rose to leave the room.

* * *

For the next week, by silent agreement, Hetty and Jared limited their conversations to his speech in Parliament. Neither mentioned his past deception or the fact his accent now matched his extensive vocabulary. It was not British, of course, as Hetty told Mr. Norton, but it was quite pleasing to the ear. She didn't add that she found it excessively pleasing.

Mr. Norton, whether by his own initiative or Jared's request, was often underfoot. When he was not, Sanders found numerous reasons to enter whichever room Hetty and Jared happened to be occupying. Their days together were shortened by Hetty, who judiciously retired immediately after dining each evening.

This act of cowardice or wisdom—neither she nor Jared cared to analyze the point—made for long, solitary evenings for both of them. By the second night, Jared found it unbearable, so he left the house for the nightlife of London's lower gambling establishments. He managed to lose a great deal of money, drink copiously, and find a measure of relief from the terrible sadness which enveloped him each time he thought of Hetty's leaving him.

For Hetty, the hours alone should have allowed her time to read all the books she had amassed during her busy days teaching Jared how to go on in London's strict Society. Unfortunately, her concentration was nonexistent, and her evenings consisted of blocks of time spent staring into space, punctuated by bouts of tears.

Hetty privately admitted she had made the appalling

mistake of falling deeply in love with the Marquess Winter. She knew he had tricked her, had probably laughed at her. But she had been given the privilege of seeing behind his mischievous boyish charm. Beneath all that was an intelligent, considerate man, the type of man she had dreamed of throughout her solitary life.

Ironic, she told the flames in the fireplace that warmed her bedchamber, that she had spent her eligible years being so painfully shy around strangers. She had been unable to find pleasure in any man's company, unable to fall in love. Now that she had the confidence to be herself and to fall in love, she was very much on the shelf and completely ineligible.

She thought her heart might break.

On the morning of Jared's speech, Hetty looked up from the breakfast she had been pretending to eat to find Jared standing in the doorway, silent and frowning.

"Good morning," she said softly.

"Good morning," he replied, crossing carefully to his place.

Sanders appeared, a cup of hot coffee in hand.

"Will you be requiring anything else, my lord?" he asked.

Jared waved him away without speaking.

While continuing to push her food about her plate, Hetty peeked at Jared, noticing he winced with each clink of silver against the plate. She expelled a censorious sigh.

Jared peered over his cup, his frown deepening.

"You were out late last night again," she said.

"And you are not eating properly," he returned. "You will become ill."

"Like you?" she asked pertly, quickly dropping her gaze to her plate and resuming the maddening assault on Jared's jangled nerves.

His hand snaked across the table and stilled her fork.

"Would you mind not doing that?" he said bluntly.

Hetty melted into his bloodshot blue eyes, his touch paralyzing any effort to reply, to pretend this was a normal conversation between normal people.

Pretend, she commanded herself. *Pretend this is not the last time you will sit across from him at the table.* Tears pooled in her eyes. Jared's grasp tightened. He lifted her hand to his lips.

She shook her head, the movement causing a tear to spill onto her cheek. Slowly, Jared reached out and brushed the tear away, his touch feather soft against her skin.

With a ragged breath, Hetty freed her hand. Mumbling an excuse, she rose and hurried out of the room.

"More coffee, my lord?" said the butler, who had witnessed the entire episode.

"No, thank you, Sanders," said Jared slowly. Half groaning, half laughing, he commented, "I should not have touched her hand. It won't happen again."

The butler sniffed and continued to loudly remove the dishes. Feeling he deserved all the pain he could bear, Jared didn't reproach the servant. Finally, Sanders cleared his throat.

"You may speak your mind, Sanders, though I daresay you will only be repeating what I have already said to myself. But go ahead. I deserve your reprimand."

Sanders straightened, abandoning his task. His frail body at attention, he said, "I have served my lady's family all my life, my lord. She is a fine woman, and I have seen her suffer because she could not be like other ladies, carefree and giddy. At the slightest cruelty, whether to man or beast, she would champion the underdog, despite the gossip it brought down on her. I heard Mr. Norton telling you she was no longer suitable for Society. The way I see it, my lord, any Society that would shun my lady is not worth much."

Jared sat up, a thoughtful frown replacing his disconsolate mien. A tiny ray of hope fought its way into his heart as he considered the old servant's intelligence.

Why not? he thought. He cared nothing for this Society Hetty and Norton continually preached about. What did he care if they disapproved of his actions? He and Hetty didn't have to remain under its decay. They could go away, just like his mother and father had.

Why shouldn't he marry her? What difference could it make? If she couldn't bear to listen to the gossip their odd alliance would cause, he would take her back to the United States.

He would go up those stairs and tell her immediately. Hang the title and the fortune! Let his cousin Casper have it all!

Whistling, he headed up the stairs, his pace slowing

as he neared Hetty's door. She had looked so forlorn at breakfast. He reached for the latch but hesitated.

No, not now, he told himself. *Wait until there is time for kisses. If I tell her now, I doubt I will go to Parliament at all! For that matter, if I so much as see her, I shall probably forget everything I am supposed to say, and she worked too hard for me to disappoint her.*

But to see her there . . . I almost wish she would wait here until I can come home and sweep her into my arms!

But she looked so sad, he thought. *I'll just give her a hint before I leave.*

"Molly, I will wear the gray today, I think," said Hetty, stepping from the bath.

"And you'll be wanting your hat with the veil, miss. I'll go and brush it."

"No, I will wear the matching gray bonnet as well."

"But, miss . . ." began the maid. Then she nodded and went about her work, muttering under her breath about the dangers of forgetting what was due to one's position.

After enduring several moments of this, Hetty said tartly, "I am almost thirty years old, Molly. I do not need you to tell me what to do anymore. There is nothing improper about a lady attending a session of Parliament, as long as she sits in the Ladies' Gallery, which I have every intention of doing. No one need know I am there to hear Lord Winter. Now, bring me some tea and biscuits, if you please. I will have no time for luncheon. And while I am out, please attend to moving my things back to Cavendish Square."

The maid, who had been with Hetty since her nursery days, muttered her way out of the room.

Hetty sat down on the bench in front of the dressing table and pulled her hair out of the tight chignon she had worn to breakfast. She ran a brush through the soft curls, her mind wandering.

When she heard the knock on the door, she waited for Molly to enter. Realizing it was not her maid, she bade the visitor come in, pulling her wrapper closed at the throat when Jared stepped into the room.

"My lord," she said, not rising for fear her attire would not properly cover her, and unsure of the strength of her own self-control.

"Hetty, I have been thinking it might be better if you didn't come today," he said, remaining beside the door, trying to force his eager gaze to the floor, but having very little success. She was fairly spilling out of the thin garment, he thought appreciatively.

"If that is what you wish, Jared," she said quietly, hoping her voice did not betray her distress, and praying her tears would wait until he had gone.

"Not what I wish, but what would be wiser, my dear. We wouldn't want anyone to guess how well acquainted we are."

"Very well," she managed, turning her back to the door and stifling a bitter laugh. "I should congratulate myself, I suppose. The pupil has surpassed the student. I have done a superb job of teaching you to obey the dictates of Society over what one truly desires."

"Hetty," said Jared, striding across the room. His fingers touched her shoulders with a staccato stroke before he recalled himself and moved away again. At the door, he said simply, "Very well. If you wish to come, do so. I would enjoy knowing I had an ally watching over me. When this is behind me, we must talk."

Hetty whirled around, but the door was already closing. Her movements jerky, she continued brushing her hair, but her mind raced from one possibility to the next.

What could they possibly say to each other? Both of them knew their time together was at an end. Unless, of course, he had decided to offer her a *carte blanche*. The unthinkable crossed Hetty's mind at this possibility, and she put away the idea quickly. Her self-respect wouldn't allow her to accept such an arrangement . . . would it?

Surely he cared for her too much to insult her so. He probably just meant to send her away, she told herself firmly. Perhaps he planned to arrange a pension for her, from a grateful employer. *Please, please,* she prayed, *do not let that be it. It would be easier to survive a cold dismissal than that!*

But what if he meant he wanted her to remain, that he couldn't let her go?

"Here's yer tea and biscuits, miss," said Molly, entering with a tray.

"Never mind, Molly, take the tray away. I couldn't eat a bite!" said Hetty.

The Houses of Parliament, especially the House of Lords, was not, as one might suppose, the backdrop for elegance and wit. Though some of the members might express themselves with eloquence, others appeared incapable of rational thought, much less speech.

Hetty watched nervously from the Ladies' Gallery as Jared entered the room, deep in conversation with someone she did not recognize. *Really,* thought Hetty, *I have been away from Society far too long. There was a time when I knew everyone.*

She felt someone staring and looked back to discover a sharp-eyed matron studying her. With the cold nod she had once perfected to depress the attentions of toadeaters, Hetty turned back to the room, watching Jared as he was introduced to various members on the way to his seat. She dropped her gaze when she observed two younger men with raised quizzing glasses studying her.

Then Jared lifted his eyes and winked at her. Hetty smiled, happy she had decided to come despite the curious audience surrounding her.

"My lords," intoned the man with whom Jared had entered, "I have the distinct pleasure of presenting to you, for the first time, the Marquess of Winter."

When the formal introduction finally ended, Jared stepped forward and, in his clear, pleasant tones, said, "My lords, it is my privilege to be here with you today. Three months ago, I had no idea who I really was." He paused as laughter circled the room. "But changing my name from Mr. Winter to Lord Winter did nothing to change the inner man. I do not pretend to understand all of the issues and problems which beset this nation and this House, but I promise you I shall do my best to learn."

Applause from his listeners made him pause, and he glanced at Hetty, his eyes smiling, asking her to share in these accolades he was receiving. The warmth she read there told her as clearly as spoken words that he considered her his partner in this maiden speech, that he could not have succeeded without her.

Then he was bowing and shaking hands. The applause dwindled, but Hetty didn't notice and continued to clap, rather too loudly and longer than was strictly proper. She could feel the matron's eyes burning into her back. The two men lifted their quizzing glasses again and stared with relentless insolence.

Hetty rose and left the gallery, her pace slow and proper, though her heart was pounding in her throat. The impossibility of her situation was borne in on her, and she fought tears as she entered the hackney cab. Wiping the tears away, she watched for Jared's exit.

There he was, tall and magnificent, his dark hair glistening in the sunlight. Suddenly, the sharp-nosed matron marched up to him and tapped him on the shoulder. Behind her was a slight young man with a harassed air about him.

Casper Golightly! thought Hetty, *Jared's cousin.* And the matron was his mother, of course. Hetty frowned as she watched the matron present one plump cheek for her newfound nephew to kiss. She mistrusted that syrupy smile on Mrs. Golightly's face.

Another man joined them, this one almost as tall and broad-shouldered as Jared. The other cousin,

Sylvester Perdue. Again, Jared greeted this new relative with apparent affability.

Recalling what Norton had said about the cousins challenging Jared's right to the title, Hetty whispered, "Be careful. Be very careful, Jared."

"Wot was that, miss? You ready to go?" asked her driver.

"In a moment." She watched as Jared turned away to accept the congratulations of another member.

Mrs. Golightly took this opportunity to give a significant nod in Jared's direction as she prodded her son with her umbrella. Watching the woman, Hetty shivered.

Other members began to gather around Jared, shaking his hand and drawing him away from his newfound family. Jared tried to disengage himself from the man who had introduced him in the House of Lords, but it was evident his efforts were not meeting with success. Hetty heard a reference to White's and smiled. Her pupil was being taken into the fold.

"Take me home, driver. South Audley Street."

Hetty made her way to the jeweler's shop, Rundell and Bridges, to pick up the watch she had purchased for Jared. She flipped open the case and read the inscription, smiling mistily.

By the time she reached Audley Street, Hetty was in a happier frame of mind. She would warn Jared to be wary of his two cousins, who stood to gain everything if anything should happen to him. She reminded herself Jared was not the innocent she had thought him at first. He could take care of himself.

Hurrying into the house, Hetty had every intention

of changing into her prettiest gown, ordering Sanders to chill a bottle of champagne, and greeting Jared, when he arrived, with a congratulatory toast.

"Miss! Miss!" intoned the agitated butler, stopping her at the foot of the stairs. "Miss, I thought you would never return!"

"What is it, Sanders?" she asked, taking his elbow to steady him. Before the butler could speak, another sound assailed her ears.

"Why, you must be that teacher Mr. Norton was told me about this morning! Miss Thompson, is it? I am Mrs. Winter—or should I say Lady Winter?" asked a vision in white who was draped across the doorway of the salon.

The front door opened, and Jared stood in the threshold, his glassy eyes seeing only Hetty—Hetty, waiting for him. Crossing the hall in three steps, he swept her into his arms, planted a warm kiss on her lips, and began singing a lively tune as he waltzed her around the entryway. The first turn brought the other woman into his line of vision.

Astonished, his mouth dropped open and his arms fell, leaving Hetty without the necessary support to keep her stunned body upright. Her eyes, the only part of her still capable of action, shifted from one to the other, taking in the flash of recognition in Jared's eyes, the spark of pleasure upon seeing this woman.

"Angel," Jared said, sealing Hetty's fate.

Hetty sank to the floor, senseless.

Seven

For virtue hath this better lesson taught,
Within myself to seek my only hire,
Desiring nought but how to kill desire.
— *Sir Philip Sidney*

"Send for her maid," called Jared as he bent to retrieve Hetty, picking her up like a rag doll. He took
her into the salon and gently deposited her on the sofa.

He grabbed Angel by the wrist and dragged her to
the study where he and Hetty had passed so many
enjoyable hours in learning and conversation.

Shoving his unwelcome visitor into a chair, he hovered over her and demanded, "What in bloody hell
are you trying to pull?"

Angel covered her eyes with a lacy handkerchief
and began to wail. Jared spat out a curse and handed
her his handkerchief.

Her eyes bright and clear, she cried, "I thought
you'd be happy to see me, Jared! You know how I feel
about you!"

"Angel, you couldn't have come at a worse time."

He leaned against the large desk, his expression cold and dispassionate. His head was spinning. He wished he had not gone to White's to celebrate before returning home. If he had come straight home, he might have avoided Angel and her machinations.

The vixen sniffed and buried her face in his handkerchief again before mumbling, "But I love you, Jared."

"Love me? Of all the infernal lies! You have never loved me, Angel!"

"That's not true, Jared! And now that you are this Lord Winter person, we can afford to be together!"

Jared laughed, a bitter sound devoid of humor.

Hetty, roused from her stupor, was being supported by Sanders and Molly to the stairs when she heard the muffled sound. Her world was crashing down about her ears, and he was laughing!

Lifting her chin, she said quietly, "Molly, pack my things."

"I already did, Miss, and sent them on. You told me to before you left to listen to his lordship's speech, remember?"

"Of course. How fortuitous," she said ironically, turning back toward the front door. "Then hail a hackney for me, Sanders. We are going home." As she passed the table in the hall, she slipped the jeweler's box from her pocket and placed it on the silver salver.

In the study, Jared rounded on his visitor. "That's all you ever cared about, money. You used me even when I was little more than a boy. You used my house to set up your gambling hall and whatever else went on."

"How can you say so? I fell in love with you the first minute I saw you!" exclaimed the aging beauty.

"Now what would an experienced woman of thirty want with a youth of twenty? It couldn't have been my house so conveniently located near the clubs," he said.

Angel rose, moving to his side and slipping her arms around his neck. Her voice sultry, she whispered, "I could show you what I really wanted, if you would let me."

Jared removed her arms and walked behind the desk.

"I didn't want you then, Angel, and I don't want you now. I appreciated your, er, sympathy when I first returned to New Orleans after finding my parents and brother dead, but it was a mistake. We agreed at the time. I was a boy, and I was in pain. Otherwise . . ."

"I know, Jared. But you must admit, the arrangement we had benefitted both of us. The men flocked to me, and they gambled with you. You enjoyed yourself. I know you did! And you were so lucky!"

"And you had a place to entertain your gentlemen friends—or should I say clients?"

"Now you are being hateful," whined Angel. "What's so terrible about my coming here? Don't I deserve a share of whatever it is you have going?"

"Ah, now we get back to the crux of the matter— money. How much do you want?" he asked, turning toward the desk with unsteady tread.

Angel followed, grasping the sleeve of his coat and imploring, "Not just the money, Jared. You're in a position to do so much more for me. I remember when that repellent little man got you freed from prison. I remember what he said about your being a powerful man back here. And now I hear you've gone and addressed all of those fine lords in Congress or whatever they call it. You have come up in the world, and I want to be a part of it. I deserve to be a part of it!"

"But you are not my wife, Angel. We were once friends, and I will be happy to send you home with some money, but that is all."

"Money isn't everything, Jared, as I have come to discover over the years. A lady wants more than money."

Jared laughed, this time with a touch of amusement. "Yes, a lady needs a house, a carriage, and servants, as well as money, isn't that so?"

"Now you understand," said Angel, her smile lighting her eyes.

"Very well, Angel. I will have Norton, that repellent little man, as you called him, see to it. In the meantime, you don't mind if I send you to a hotel, do you?"

"That depends," she began suspiciously. "What kind of hotel?"

Jared laughed out loud. "If there is one thing that never changes in this world, Angel, it is your ability to cut through all the chaff and head straight to the heart of the matter. Don't worry, I'll have Sanders order a hackney and carry you to the very best hotel in all of London."

Angel threw her arms around his neck, and Jared quickly disengaged himself.

"Provided, of course, you do not use my name in vain again," he cautioned.

"What name was that, my lord?" She laughed.

"Exactly. Now I must see if I can salvage what is left of my reputation with Miss Thompson."

Jared squared his shoulders and walked toward the door, but Angel's words made him pause.

"You really love her, don't you?"

"You could tell that?" he asked, a self-deprecating grin transforming his grim appearance.

"It's in your eyes, Jared. I once wished I would see you look at me like that, but you never did. This Miss Thompson is a very lucky woman."

"Thank you, Angel. Good-bye."

A quick check of the empty salon sent Jared upstairs, one hand leaning heavily on the banister. *My God,* he thought, *these English lords are hardheaded men.* He would have to remember not to "take wine" with them again.

He reached the landing and lumbered down the hall to Hetty's sitting room. Empty! Frowning, he retraced his steps, his heart starting to pound in agitation when he noticed Sanders was not in his usual post by the front door.

"Sanders!" he roared, causing the lone footman in the hall to jump to attention. "Sanders!"

"Pardon, my lord, but Mr. Sanders has just left."

Jared made it down the steps and rounded on the trembling servant, his fists clenched. "What the deuce are you talking about?"

"Mr. Sanders, my lord. He went with the mistress and her maid in a hackney cab."

His teeth clenched, too. Jared growled, "Where the devil did they go?"

"I couldn't say, my lord. I heard Miss Thompson say something about going home."

Jared's fist crashed against the wall, sending plaster everywhere and the footman running. The front door opened, and Jared looked up, his hopeful expression fading to one of black despair as Norton stepped nervously into the hall. Angel appeared from the study.

"What has happened, my lord?" asked Norton. "I thought your speech went very well."

"Blast the damned speech, and blast you, Norton!" Jared turned and strode to the study. Pushing past Angel, he went straight to the decanters and poured a full measure of Scotch, throwing it down his throat and grunting with satisfaction.

"Good afternoon, Mrs. Grant." Norton mopped his brow and gave the visitor a quick bow.

"Good afternoon, Mr. Norton," Angel said seductively, unable to address a man in any other manner.

"What happened?" whispered Norton, watching in alarm as Jared poured another glass.

"I'm not dead, you know," Jared said with a sneer. "You can address me."

"Of course, my lord. Very well, what happened?"

"You tell him, Angel. You're such an integral part of this little charade. You tell him." Jared finished off that glass and poured another before flopping onto the sofa.

Norton sidled to the tray of decanters and poured two small glasses of sherry. He moved the Scotch out of Jared's reach before handing one sherry to Angel and sipping from the other himself.

"I'm afraid my arrival upset Miss Thompson. At

least, I suppose it did," said Angel, her eyes wide and innocent.

Jared snorted, muttered, "Just a little," and finished the drink he held.

"Anyway, she fainted. Perhaps she hadn't eaten anything." The seductress fluttered her eyes for Norton's benefit. "That sometimes happens to me when I forget to eat, you know."

"Oh, for pity's sake! You told her we were married! What was she supposed to think?" snapped Jared, rising again, but none too steadily. He bypassed the decanters and went to the desk, drawing out pen and paper.

"What do you call those men, those investigators that track down criminals?" he asked, his words beginning to slur.

"Bow Street Runner?" asked Norton.

Jared nodded and began to write.

"But my lord, there is no need to send for them!"

"Why is that?" asked Jared, his eyes drooping closed for a second before they flew open again. He blinked rapidly several times.

"If Miss Thompson has gone home, I know where she lives!" said Norton.

"Why didn't you say so? Let's go!"

Jared rose, clasping the edge of the desk to steady himself. Taking a step toward Norton, he miscalculated and tripped, sprawling across the desk. He lifted his head, mumbled something incoherent, and passed out.

"I'll take care of him," said Angel. Winking coyly at the solicitor, she added, "I know just what to do."

"I'll call the footman so we can get him to bed, Mrs. Grant." Norton scurried from the study.

Gibbons hurriedly turned down the bed, and they tucked Jared in. Norton fussed over him, shaking his head and clucking like a mother hen.

"I never realized what a good-hearted man you are, Mr. Norton," Angel said, smiling sweetly at him.

Tobias Norton flushed with pleasure and stammered, "I am only doing my job, Mrs. Grant."

"Call me Angel, won't you?" she said. Taking him by the arm, she led him out of Jared's bedroom and down the stairs to the cozy study.

"I really think I should go to see Miss Thompson," said Norton. "You know, Mrs. Grant—I mean, Angel—when you came by my office to discover Lord Winter's direction, I had no idea your arrival would cause such a contretemps."

"I know, Mr. Norton, and I feel so embarrassed. I meant it as a little joke, but Miss Thompson didn't give me a chance to explain."

"I understand, my dear," said Norton, looking up at her with adoring eyes.

"Now, why don't we have a little supper? Are you hungry? I am positively famished," she drawled, raising her shoulders and crossing her arms. The effect this pose had on Norton was prodigious. He nodded, incapable of speech.

Hetty also spent the remainder of the afternoon tucked up in bed, a raging headache rendering any action impossible. She knew she would have to face her broken heart on the morrow, but the headache gave her the excuse to put off the inevitable. Molly had prescribed a stout dose of laudanum, but Hetty refused, knowing she would need a clear head when she woke and decided what to do next. What did one do after making an utter cake of oneself? she wondered, frowning as the question and short-lived tears made her head pound viciously.

It was dusk when Molly crept into the darkened chamber and, as if speaking to someone who had just lost a loved one, said softly, "Miss, your brother has come to call."

"Tell him to go away, Molly. I can't face him today."

"Very good, miss," said the maid, leaving the cozy room silently, waiting until she was in the corridor before she blew her nose and wiped her eyes. She and Sanders had harbored such hopes for their dear mistress!

"Well?" The Duke of Bosworth broke off his conversation with Sanders when Molly returned to the salon.

"She's that sick, your grace. If you could come back tomorrow, she said she would see you."

Harry might be a duke, but he was also a brother, and a twin brother at that. He refused to take no for an answer and, assuring the loyal maid he would be quiet, went to Hetty's bedside.

"I don't remember a headache ever keeping you down, my dear girl," he said, peering at her through the gloom. The window curtains were drawn against the late afternoon sun, and though there was a stout fire against the chill, no candles burned.

Hetty opened her eyes and smiled weakly.

"You don't mind if I just sit here and keep you company for a while?" When she didn't reply, he settled himself in a chair beside the bed and began to hum quietly.

After several moments, Hetty opened one eye and said crossly, "Always lording it over me, aren't you, that you can carry a tune and I can't."

"Ah, but you have hidden talents, my dear."

"I don't think so," she said miserably.

"Of course you do. You can inspire the most incredible devotion in your servants. Not one of them here would tell me where you had gone this past month."

"There was no need. I wrote to tell you I was visiting friends down south."

"Hetty, the only friends you ever visit are us. Where have you been?"

She pressed a hand to her forehead as the pounding increased. "It doesn't matter. I am home now."

"Good God!" exclaimed her brother, rising and pacing for a moment. "Hetty, never tell me the rumors were true!"

Rising up on her elbows, Hetty retorted, "Since I have no idea what the rumors may have been—and if I did, I would have enough sense to ignore them—then I can neither confirm or deny them." With a groan, she subsided into the pillows.

"I am a brute!" said the duke. Then more gently, he added, "Go to sleep. We will speak of this tomorrow."

"I can hardly wait," came the caustic reply.

But even in sleep, Hetty could not evade her romantic dreams. She was chasing Jared, running as fast as she could, but her legs and feet would not cooperate. She was mired in the mud, screaming his name, but either he couldn't hear her or wouldn't answer. She awoke to tears running down her face and a gentle shaking of her shoulders.

"Harry?" she said, her voice hoarse with sleep.

"Yes, you were crying. Here, blow your nose," he commanded, giving her a soft handkerchief.

When she had settled back on the pillows, she looked up and smiled at her twin.

"Thank you for staying, Harry," she said softly. "I needed a shoulder to cry on."

"Go back to sleep," he replied gruffly, fussing with the covers.

When he had settled back in the bedside chair, and his face was lost in the darkness again, she asked quietly, "What were the rumors?"

"Not rumors, really. One or two people mentioned they had seen you about town with a man, some stranger."

He didn't ask, but she knew his curiosity, possibly even anger, was burning to know what she had been doing. She owed it to Harry and Amy to let them know she had not been doing anything clandestine, but a complete confession would be too painful.

"That was a man I was giving elocution lessons to, Harry. That's all. It was all rather confidential, I'm afraid."

"So you don't plan to tell me who it was," said Harry.

Hetty shook her head.

"Very well, my dear, I won't press you. I wasn't really worried that you had, er, well, you know."

"Taken a slip on the shoulder?" she supplied with a hollow laugh.

"Language!" said Harry in his best imitation of their terrifying Aunt Mary. He leaned closer so she could share his grin. "Young ladies whose speech belongs in a stable usually end up in one."

Hetty giggled. "You do that a little too well, Harry."

"Baggage," he said, the smile fading as their eyes met in complete understanding.

After a few moments, when her brother was once again enveloped in obscurity, Hetty said, "I want to go home, Harry."

She knew he was nodding in the darkness.

Harry replied, "Tomorrow."

"What the devil do you mean, I can't call on her!" snarled Jared over a cup of steaming coffee.

Norton said firmly, "I said you can't call on her this early, my lord. It is only nine o'clock. Miss Thompson, after such an eventful day yesterday, is very probably sleeping late."

Jared didn't want to admit that the solicitor was making sense, nor did he want to sit around, waiting patiently for the proper time to call. His head was throbbing, his temper was short, and he wanted action.

"Ten o'clock, my lord, is the earliest you should call. And I suggest you bathe and have your man shave you first," said Norton, before playing his trump card. "Miss Thompson, were she still here, would agree."

"Killjoy," grumbled Jared, but he settled back in his chair, cradling his coffee cup with trembling hands.

"Your man could also mix up something for those tremors, my lord," offered Norton.

Jared set the cup on the table and glared at the solicitor, who took it in good part and concentrated on his own breakfast.

"Good morning, gentlemen," sang Angel, floating into the room, passing behind Norton's chair and allowing the flowing sleeve on her dressing gown to slide across his cheek.

"Good morning, Angel." Jared's eyes lighted with amusement as he watched the earnest older man flush with pleasure. "What did you find to occupy your time last night?"

She joined them at the table, her plate filled with a hearty breakfast of eggs and sausages. She bestowed a coy look on Norton before saying airily, "Oh, we filled our hours with delightful conversation. Didn't we, Tobias?"

Norton squirmed uncomfortably in his chair before seeming to come to a decision. Throwing a challenging glance at Jared, he turned to Angel, saying, "Yes, my dear, quite delightful conversation."

Jared chuckled and shook his head, an action which he immediately regretted. Rising, he excused himself and made his way up the stairs to have Gibbons draw him a hot bath and mix up that "something" Norton had mentioned.

Gibbons had the hot water waiting for him, and

Jared slipped into the bath with a sigh. The valet handed him a vile smelling mixture that tasted surprisingly good, and by the time Jared was dressed, he felt almost human.

"Excuse me, my lord. The footman handed this to me last night, but I decided it would be best to wait until today to give it to you."

Puzzled, Jared unwrapped the package, his eyes misting as he opened the watch and read the inscription.

"Where did it come from?" he asked quietly.

"The footman saw Miss Thompson slip it onto the table before she left."

"Thank you, Gibbons," said Jared, slipping the watch into his pocket and fastening the fob to his waistcoat. He prayed it would bring him luck.

It was well after eleven o'clock before he and Norton arrived at Hetty's house in Cavendish Square. The solicitor had been unsure of the house number and had had to return to his office to recover it. Though he was a volcano of impatience, Jared had managed to say nothing.

As the carriage rolled to a stop, Jared jumped down and ran up the short flight of stone steps before Norton's call made him pause.

"There is no knocker, my lord!"

Jared turned back to the door. The frowning solicitor joined him in beating on the door. After several minutes, just when they were about to give up, the door inched open.

"Hmm?" said Ned, the gardener.

"Where is Miss Thompson? I must see her," said Jared.

Ned looked him up and down. Then he slowly shook his head and began to close the door. Jared thrust his foot into the aperture and put his shoulder to the wood, forcing it wide.

"I said I must see your mistress. I'm not leaving until I do." He stepped into the hall and stole a glance at the salon. "Hetty! Hetty!" Only silence returned his greeting. Frowning, he noticed the Holland covers shrouding the furniture.

"Mistress bain't 'ere."

"That's 'my lord' to you, my good man. How long has she been gone?" asked Norton. "Your mistress, I mean."

" 'ours an' 'ours, sir. Couldn't say where. Th' quality don't tell me nothink," said Ned, enjoying his role.

Jared studied the man closely. He fancied he could smell trickery. The man couldn't be as ignorant as he claimed. Yet hadn't he done the same thing to Hetty?

Guilt and regret welled up in Jared's breast, and he grabbed the servant by the collar and shook him. Both Ned and Norton clawed at his grip, shouting their protests, but Jared's impotent rage made him blind to reason.

"Awright!" yelled the servant, his feet dangling in the air. Jared relaxed his grip, and Ned scrambled away, putting the solicitor between him and the madman.

"I really can't say, milord. Mistress told me not to tell."

Jared took a deep breath. Speaking though clenched

teeth, he ground out painfully, fearful of the response he would hear, "You can tell me, friend."

Slinking farther away from the marquess's strong hands, Ned said, "I'm sorry, milord, but mistress said as how I warn't to tell anybody, 'specially a tall, foreign lord."

"I can pay you well," said Jared.

"Ain't th' money, milord. I just can't say."

Jared rounded suddenly on the solicitor. "What about you, Norton? You said her family was powerful. Surely you know who they are."

"I only surmised as much from what I heard. I'm afraid I never learned the name. The people I dealt with were much too discreet, if they even knew themselves," said the solicitor sadly.

Jared turned, touching the covered furniture and sending a cloud of dust into the air. It had been that way for some time. Hetty may have returned to her house yesterday, but she must have had no intention of remaining. She had wanted only to escape from him. What a lowering thought. The clock over the mantle began to chime the hour.

Jared extracted the watch Hetty had given to him. He opened it, checking its accuracy, but his eyes fell on that inscription again.

"Aimez, aimez, tout le reste n'est rien."

"My lord?"

"Love, love, all else is nothing," murmured Jared, shaking his head.

With a sigh, he turned to Norton, saying with forced composure, "I believe we were going to open up that town house of mine. I think I would like to go see it."

"Of course, my lord."

Two days later, Jared was installed in the spacious town house that had belonged to his family for several generations. Norton took special pride in watching his master cross the threshold of his new home for the first time. For Jared, the building seemed cold and uninviting, but he had pledged to himself to become the marquess Winter in truth, so he accepted this house and its legion of well-trained servants as his due.

Though it was only the first of March and London was very thin of company, the invitations began to roll in. Jared found he could fill many lonely hours by accepting all of these invitations, much to the delight of his hostesses.

His cousin Casper Golightly—a harmless fribble, Jared had decided—was often to be found on his doorstep, a willing companion should Jared need a guide on his forays into the Polite World.

Norton, once he had seen Jared settled and occupied, seldom visited, explaining that his constant presence would serve only to limit his lordship.

Jared sent to Bow Street and hired one of their finest to track down Hetty. He didn't allow himself to dwell on the loss he felt since her departure, but the pain assailed him at the oddest times. Meals were the worst. Eating at the long table all alone was nearly intolerable. He longed to be able to turn to his right and share his thoughts with her.

In the past, Jared had never had trouble making friends, but there was now a reserve about him which kept strangers, which meant everyone he met, at arm's length. His cousin Casper put him up for membership in White's and he was accepted, but Jared rarely attended, preferring to accompany Casper to the less savory gambling hells where no one held expectations of him.

Rising at noon one day, Jared was surprised to be informed by his very proper butler, Martin, that he had callers—not only his cousin Casper, but his aunt and other cousin, as well.

He was in no hurry to join his condescending aunt, but he was curious about Sylvester, whom he had met after his speech in Parliament. Calling for Gibbons, he dressed quickly.

When Jared entered the salon, his aunt intoned regally, "You have been a stranger too long, nephew. That is not how things are done here in England." She was dressed all in purple, a color that ill-matched her reddish complexion.

"As you know, I only arrived in England a short while ago, Aunt Honoria," said Jared, dragging her name out because he knew it would annoy her.

"Sylvester has come with me to see that you go about and meet the right people. Isn't that so, Sylvester?"

Casper pushed off from the mantle and stalked to the window, his bottom lip protruding slightly.

"Quite right, Aunt Honoria," said Sylvester, a darkly

handsome man who closely matched Jared in size. He extended two fingers to Jared, who ignored them.

"I forget. Just how is it we are related?" asked Jared, enjoying being obtuse.

"Sylvester's mother, my youngest sister, died when he was born. My brother, the late marquess, and I raised him at Winterhurst."

"Casper, too, I presume," said Jared, smiling in the direction of his sulking cousin.

"Of course. My late husband passed away at the early age of thirty of the apoplexy. We were quite a happy little family," added his aunt.

Casper coughed and muttered, "I never liked Winterhurst. Daresay you won't either, Jared. It's nothing but a mausoleum."

"Perhaps, but I'm looking forward to seeing the place, I must admit," said Jared.

"But you can't leave London now!" exclaimed his aunt, throwing her hands up dramatically.

"Why not?" he asked.

"Because Sylvester will be so disappointed if he is denied the treat of showing you the town, introducing you to all the right people," said Mrs. Golightly, with what Jared supposed passed for a smile.

"I've taken Jared all over the place," grumbled Casper.

His mother fixed him with a minatory stare, and he subsided, chewing on his thumbnail and scowling.

"Be happy to show you about, old man," said Sylvester. "London is quite thin of company at the moment, of course, but there are always entertainments to be found once you know where to look for them."

"Kind of you to offer," said Jared, "but I seem to be doing all right in the invitation department."

He indicated the stack of stiff white cards resting on the table nearest his aunt. The nosy matron picked them up and shuffled through them, her throat and cheeks becoming suffused in red.

"Unexceptional," she managed to choke out.

"We thought so, didn't we, Casper?"

His cousin brightened and agreed, ducking his head when his mama quelled him with another frown.

"Yes, well, I really should be going. Come along, boys," she said. "Let me know when you are ready to make the journey to Winterhurst, nephew, and I will accompany you. You will need to be introduced to the servants and the tenants, and who better to do so than I?"

She caught her breath, and Jared hurriedly bade them good-bye before she could launch into another topic.

But Jared did not let his aunt know his intentions when he and Norton set out at the end of the week to Hampshire to visit Winterhurst. The steward, a capable, affable man named Pearson, welcomed Jared's arrival, taking him to each tenant's farm on the estate and introducing the new lord and master.

The house was quite old and spacious. He felt immediately and surprisingly at home. When Norton introduced him to his ancestors in the family gallery,

Jared spent some time contemplating the picture of his grandmother holding his infant father in her lap. His uncle, the late Marquess Winter, stood by her side, a lad of seven or eight. The woman's smile was sweet and loving. Jared could only wonder what would have happened if she had lived to see her two sons become adults.

The Winterhurst estate was not large, but it prospered. Norton explained that Pearson was such a good steward, the land provided well for both its tenants and the family.

Jared had planned to stay at Winterhurst two weeks, but the unexpected arrival of his Aunt Honoria sent him scurrying back to London. His thick-skinned aunt declared she would return also and so ruined a very pleasant journey for Norton, who had to ride inside the carriage with her. Jared, except to escape a brief shower, rode on horseback.

Back in London, the Season was beginning. The number of stiff white envelopes arriving at his town house trebled. Still, Jared found little pleasure in his crowded life.

It was the small things which made him retreat from this new life. While attending Lady Falworthy's ball one evening, he noticed an absurd little man waltzing on tiptoe with a tall blond girl. Their efforts at conversation were laughable. He wished he could tell Hetty about it. She would have been amused, he thought dismally. And then there had been the dramatic quarrel between two young lovers whose betrothal had just been announced. . . .

Returning home that evening, Jared found sleep im-

possible. He vowed to do something more to find
Hetty. The fellow from Bow Street hadn't turned up
anything yet. Perhaps he would hire another runner.
Surely between the two of them, they would be able
to find her. And if, when she was found, she didn't
wish to continue their friendship, he would learn to
live with it.

Somehow.

Early the next morning, Jared was riding his huge
bay through the park as usual. The skies were blue
and cold, and his breath blew like smoke in the wind.

His greatcoat was fastened to the top, its three capes
protecting him from the elements. A wool scarf was
tied around his neck and pulled up over his mouth
and cheeks. But the gelding was restless, stepping
sideways despite the gallop they had had when they
first entered the park.

"Come on, big fellow, let's go home. It's too demmed cold out here for either one of us. We both
should . . ."

Crack!

"What in the . . ." Jared leaped off the gelding, diving for the ground, waiting, every nerve standing on
end.

The wind whistling through the trees was the only
sound he heard. Still, he didn't move.

Suddenly, on the cold ground beneath his cheek, he
could feel the drumming of hooves, and he jumped to
his feet, whirling in the direction of the noise.

The horse and rider were too far away to catch, too

far away to recognize. All he could distinguish was the horse's flaxen tail whipping in the wind.

He hopped onto the large gelding's back and sped across the park to the trees where the assailant had disappeared. The dead grass was packed down as if the person had been waiting for some time, pacing up and down to keep warm. Dismounting again, he discovered a ball that had fallen to the ground.

Jared pocketed the charge and remounted, turning his horse to home. He kept looking over his shoulder, the hair on the back of his neck standing at attention.

Jared looked up from the papers scattered across his desk when the Bow Street Runner entered his study.

"You wanted to see me, milord?" The man shuffled from one foot to the other.

"Have a seat, Taggert," said Jared, pointing at one of two chairs across from him.

"Thank you, milord. I was comin' tomorrow to report to you anyway."

"Have you any news for me?" asked Jared eagerly.

"No, milord, I'm afraid not. The only ones who might know your Miss Thompson's real name and family are those servants still there in Cavendish Square, an' you know they're not talkin'."

"Never mind that for now, Taggert. There is another matter, equally delicate, which I want you to look into for me." Jared pulled the pistol ball out of his pocket and handed it to the runner, telling him all the details of his dangerous morning ride. "He had to have dropped it. Otherwise, it would have been ground into the earth."

"That's logical," said the runner, holding the ball up and studying it. "Pretty common sort of shot, milord."

"I don't consider it common when it, or rather another like it, was aimed at me!" exclaimed Jared.

He didn't like looking over his shoulder every time he left his house. When he left New Orleans, he thought he had left behind his havey-cavey life and acquaintances. England was supposed to be civilized.

"Who's th' next to inherit after you, milord? Oftentimes, that's th' culprit."

"My cousin, Casper Golightly, but he doesn't seem the sort. I doubt he would have the nerve," said Jared.

"Money does funny things t' people," said the runner. "What about th' horse? Have you ever seen it before? There's not many around with that color o' tail."

Jared thought for a moment before shaking his head. "Taggert, I don't care how you do it, but I want you to find out who shot at me this morning. You can let rest the search for Miss Thompson until you do."

"Very good, milord," said the runner. "You know, milord, as I told you before, you're the one as could find Miss Thompson. It's the nobs you need t' be askin', not servants."

"The nobs?"

"You know, the gents, like you."

"Perhaps, but I wouldn't want to damage the lady's reputation by making such awkward inquiries. No, it can wait. This other matter is more urgent, I warrant.

Do not let me down this time, Taggert. It's a matter of life and death."

"I won't, milord. And I think I'll put someone on the house, just to keep an eye out."

"Good idea, but introduce me to the fellow first. I'd hate to blow his head off and then find out he was only here to protect me," said Jared, reaching into the drawer and pulling out a pair of dueling pistols.

"I trust it won't come to that, milord," said the runner.

"I don't think I'll trust anything," said Jared.

Eight

How like a winter hath my absence been
From thee, the pleasure of the fleeting year!
—Shakespeare

"I wish I were old enough for a Season now," whined Abigail, Hetty's seven-year-old niece, putting her hand inside Hetty's fur muff and parading in front of the mirror.

"I don't!" Her twin sister, Annie, rolled her eyes in distaste. "You have to dress up all the time, and there's not even a good place to ride!"

"Who cares about riding?" asked Abigail. "Unless I could have a stylish riding habit, of course!"

"Actually, there are several parks for riding, Annie. And it can be most pleasant to wear a stylish riding habit and have the handsome gentlemen vie for the best spot at your side," said Hetty, rising from her dressing table as her maid put the finishing touches on her hair. Although she had never had men vying for a place by her side, she felt certain it would have been agreeable.

Turning to her maid, Hetty said, "Thank you, Molly. I wonder if you might do a little something with the Ladies Abigail and Annie."

They surrounded the smiling maid with eager entreaties.

"Sit down, Lady Abigail. I'll do yours first, but remember, this is just for pretending. You can't go down to meet the guests with your hair up. Not until you are twenty or thirty, anyway," added the maid with a wink at her mistress.

Hetty smoothed her dark green evening gown of watered silk and blew a kiss to the girls, adjuring them to enjoy themselves. She made her way through the rambling corridors without a misstep; she knew every inch of the way.

Returning to Bosworth had been a wise decision. She felt she had regained her identity, the Hetty of old. How foolish she had been, fancying herself in love with the handsome Marquess Winter. She was not a green young miss with nothing between her ears.

At Bosworth, she could be herself again—doting aunt, loving sister, helpful sister-in-law. She would tire of this in time, she knew, and return to London to teach again. But for now, she was comforted by these familiar roles. Here, she was accepted for herself— witty but shy, introspective but selfless, and most of all, sensible.

"You are looking particularly lovely tonight, Hetty," said her sister-in-law, Amy, when Hetty entered the salon.

Joining Amy on the sofa, Hetty thanked her and nodded to the neighbors she knew.

"I have just left the girls. They are having Molly put up their hair," she said, including in her comment the squire's wife, who was seated on her left.

"They are such dear children," said Mrs. Potts.

"Thank you," said Amy. "They are the best of friends, you know. I am glad they are not identical. No one expects them to like all the same things."

"And they are both beauties," said the squire's wife. "Tell me, how are the boys?"

"Very well, they grow taller every day. I can hardly believe they are two years old already."

"They are talking," said Hetty in her best aunt's voice.

"Talking! Why, they must be terribly advanced! My dear Niles, you know, is quite a scholar, but he barely spoke before the age of three!" said Mrs. Potts.

"I believe that is a sign of high intelligence," said Hetty, remembering something she had come across in her studies on children. The comment left Mrs. Potts beaming.

"Indeed! I didn't know that!"

"Oh, yes, and I have found it to be true. My . . ." Hetty stopped, horrified at what she had been about to say—students. She stole a glance at her sister-in-law, whose alarm was conspicuous. Worse still, Mrs. Potts was the biggest gossip in the neighborhood. It didn't bear contemplation, divulging such dangerous secrets to her present audience.

Continuing with a smile, Hetty said, "Yes, I have read a great deal on the subject. I find it fascinating," she added, earning a smile of relief from Amy and a gleam of interest from Mrs. Potts.

"Really? You must tell me more, Lady Henrietta," said Mrs. Potts, leaning forward eagerly.

Looking for a distraction, Hetty saw Perry Bigglesby talking to a pretty young miss with perfect blond curls and a turned-up nose.

"Who is Mr. Bigglesby talking to?" asked Hetty.

"That is my niece, Catherine Tilbury," said the squire's wife, leaning forward and whispering, "He has spoken to my husband, you know."

"Really? How wonderful," said Hetty, feeling a rush of emotion she refused to recognize as jealousy.

"Oh, my dear Lady Henrietta, I do apologize. I had forgotten Mr. Bigglesby was your beau at one time."

"True," said Amy, hastily defending her sister-in-law from any subtle insult, "but dear Hetty finally convinced Mr. Bigglesby they would go on much better as friends."

"Really?" came the doubtful query, but the squire's wife smiled and rose, joining her niece and Perry Bigglesby.

"Thank you, Amy, but I could have managed," said Hetty.

"Yes, of course. Still, I was afraid you had forgotten how relieved you were that Perry no longer regarded you as a possible Mrs. Bigglesby!" Amy giggled.

"Hetty, you remember my old friend Roger Ponsonby," said her brother, joining them.

Hetty smiled perfunctorily at the balding gentleman with the round stomach. "Yes, of course. It has been a number of years."

"Indeed it has, Lady Henrietta. I think his grace and I were all of sixteen or seventeen the last time I visited Bosworth. I have been busy since then, but I see you are as lovely as ever," he added, smiling.

Hetty noticed his eyes, which were a pale green. They held a decided twinkle, and she was suddenly transported back to London, recalling the way Jared's eyes lighted with amusement.

Covering her inattention, she smiled brightly and inquired, "What have you been doing since then, Mr. Ponsonby?"

"Dinner, your grace," said the tall, dignified butler.

"Ladies? Gentlemen?" Harry led them from the salon to the dining room. Roger Ponsonby offered his arm to Hetty, and they soon discovered her sister-in-law had arranged for Roger to be her partner at the table. Hetty directed a suspicious glare at Amy, which she returned with a bright smile.

Surprisingly, Roger Ponsonby proved an entertaining dinner companion, neither silent nor too verbose. Hetty had to admit that Amy, and probably her brother, had done well to pair her with Mr. Ponsonby. He was a childless widower, however, and Hetty suspected all three of them of matchmaking.

"So you have been living in London," he said. "I suppose you enjoy the fast-paced life of the city."

"Actually, I live very quietly, Mr. Ponsonby. I go to the theater, but I am not involved in the usual social whirl."

He appeared relieved, then asked, "I suppose you prefer the city to the country?"

"Both have their merits. It is simply that I have a house in the city. I do not have one in the country."

"But there is Bosworth," he commented, looking

around at the elegantly appointed dining room with its papered walls and thick carpeting.

"Bosworth is my brother's home, and my sister-in-law's. I am only a guest here—a welcome guest, I trust," said Hetty.

"Of course. I didn't mean to presume," said Mr. Ponsonby. "I remember how my wife disliked my sister coming to stay when she was confined. Adele poked her nose into everything! Of course, after . . ."

Hetty placed a gloved hand over his for a second before remembering such an action might be misconstrued in this setting. She smiled and removed her hand.

"I beg your pardon," she said.

"No, no, I appreciate your expression of sympathy. My wife was a very dear lady, but it has been some time, and I should be able to speak of her passing and that of our son. Still, it is difficult. I apologize for ruining our pleasant conversation, Lady Henrietta."

"Nonsense, you didn't ruin anything. And please, if you wish to be my friend, do not call me Lady Henrietta. I much prefer Lady Hetty. It is perhaps a little casual, but I have never been able to abide the name Henrietta. I can't imagine what my father was thinking!" she said, chuckling. "If Harry and I hadn't been twins, I would have accused him of wanting me to be a boy."

"Wanting you to be a boy? Impossible!" said her dinner partner, taking his cue and returning their intimate exchange to the proper level of polite conversation.

Amy rose and led the ladies to the salon. In the

corridor, Hetty realized she had left behind her reticule and stepped back into the dining room. The gentlemen had been at their brandy and cigars for only a moment, but the room was already thick with smoke, and the discourse was decidedly more robust.

Hetty slipped in and quickly retrieved the delicately crocheted bag. As she turned to go, her attention was caught by a well-known name, "Winterhurst." She paused, unnoticed.

"Read it in the papers. I think it must have been the heir!" said the squire.

"When did it happen?" asked another man.

"It's been two, perhaps three weeks," said the squire.

"Man deserves it, if you ask me," said the squire's eldest son. "Coming back to England after all this time and taking everything. It should have gone to Golightly!"

"But the man's a fool! Golightly, I mean," said Roger Ponsonby, laughing.

"And no matter when he came, he is the rightful heir to the marquessate," said Harry.

The older men nodded in agreement. Her brother, being a duke, could have said anything and they would have agreed, Hetty thought caustically.

"I'm sure Golightly feels the same," continued Harry. "He wouldn't have tried to kill the marquess. Must have been someone else."

"Probably someone trying to rob him," said the squire.

The men turned as one as a gasp issued from Hetty's lips. Pale as a ghost, she still smiled and mumbled an apology for disturbing them, holding out her reticule like a prized pheasant by way of explanation.

Her voice shaky, she asked casually, "The new Marquess Winter? Was he hurt?"

"No, not a scratch," said the squire, turning back to the others.

Harry watched his sister's reaction, his gaze sharp and discerning. Hetty nodded to him and hurried out the door.

She knew Harry would not let it rest until he had the truth of the matter, and she simply could not face him in front of company. At the moment, Hetty was fairly certain she couldn't sustain a rational conversation with anyone.

Someone was trying to kill Jared. Did he think it was only a robber? Did he suspect his cousin was trying to kill him? He probably had no idea what a man might do for such power and money.

Hetty hurried to her room, where she scrawled a quick note to her sister-in-law, pleading the headache. Molly, sensing the urgency in her mistress's manner, carried the note downstairs personally. When she returned, Hetty was pulling out drawers and throwing the contents on the bed.

"What is it, my lady? What has happened?"

"Someone shot at Lord Winter!" she said, her eyes communicating what her voice did not.

"Who? A thief? A burglar?"

"I don't know. It may have been Golightly, his heir," said Hetty, continuing her assault on the organized room.

Molly stilled her mistress's hands and said calmly,

"You must find out, my lady. If it was someone trying to steal th' silver, then there's nothing to worry about."

The maid had Hetty's attention now, and she continued, "Besides, only think of that Mr. Golightly. Do you really think he could do such a thing? He didn't strike me as the sort who could reason out such a plan, unless he has undergone a mighty change since you knew him all those years ago."

"But . . ."

"You must find out."

"You're right, Molly. I know! I'll go downstairs to Harry's study. Someone said he had read about it in the paper. Harry may still have the newspaper with the account."

"Yes, you do that, but first, let me fix your hair. Looks like two mice have been playing in it."

"Thank you, Molly," said Hetty, sitting obediently at the dressing table.

"That's what I'm here for," said the maid.

In the mirror's reflection, Hetty viewed the disarray of the room. Wrinkling her nose in contrition, she said sheepishly, "I promise to help you straighten up when I come back." Rising, she placed a quick kiss on the soft cheek of her faithful maid.

"Go on with you, child," said Molly, flushing with gratification.

Hetty hurried down the back stairs, which emptied out close to the kitchens and to Harry's study. Slipping inside, she found the stack of papers Harry always kept on the corner of his desk, waiting for a thorough read. She picked up the first, quickly scanning each page. Putting it down, she started on the second.

"It's in the next one, I believe," said Harry, stepping into the room after Hetty had scattered the top three or four journals across the polished surface of the desk. Ignoring him, Hetty continued her search, grunting in satisfaction when she discovered the short account of the attempted robbery, as they were calling it.

"It was in the park," she said, her eyes narrowed, "not at home."

"Yes?" said her brother, pouring another glass of claret for himself. He offered her a sherry, which she tried to refuse. "It will make you appear less dead," he insisted. In answer to her frown, he added, "You are as pale as a ghost."

Hetty sipped the potent liquid, making a face. She raised her eyes to meet his. A glimmer of a smile flashed before it faded to sadness. He motioned for her join him in the matching chairs before the fire.

"How did you meet the new marquess?" he asked, the only indication that he was agitated a slight working of his jaw.

"A solicitor came to see me last November, telling me about a youth who would need my services. The position, he said, required secrecy. When he returned from New Orleans, I discovered my new pupil was not a youth," she said, her tone almost bitter. "It was Jared Winter, the new Marquess Winter."

"I see."

"It was quite straightforward, really. They wanted to wait until he was ready before springing him on the Polite World, so we worked in a small house in

London. Then last week everything became complicated, confused."

"Go on, Hetty. You'll find I listen very well. Having a wife and four children has brought me a measure of patience I didn't possess when we were growing up," said Harry. The muscles in his jaw twitched with suppressed outrage.

"I realized he had been tricking me about his horrid grammar and accent. I was so mad," she said, a fond smile playing on her lips. Then she remembered her brother and continued, "I was going to leave then, but Jared convinced me to stay. He didn't have to work very hard at it," she admitted, falling into a daydream of remembrances.

"I should have gone," she whispered at length and shivered in the suddenly cold room.

"What happened?" asked Harry, rising and turning away to poke at the glowing embers in the fireplace, giving her a chance to regain her composure.

"I helped him write his speech for the House of Lords, you know. He did such a good job. I was proud of him."

"I was there, and it was an excellent speech. That is how I knew you were in London. I saw you in the Ladies' Gallery."

"You never said so!"

"Somehow, I knew you wouldn't want to be discovered there by me. When I went back to your house that afternoon, everything was still under Holland covers, which puzzled me. Then I saw your man Ned bringing all the trunks into the house. He wouldn't explain, of course. That man's a true jewel."

"Yes, he is, except that he didn't bother to tell me you had called. I might have contrived to put up a better front if he had warned me you were in town."

"From what I could see, Hetty, nothing could have prevented that," said Harry, waiting for several moments before saying, "You needn't tell me the rest. I can guess."

He rose and moved to the door.

"I will make your excuses to Amy so she won't pester you for explanations."

"I must go to London, Harry. Immediately!"

"Very well, in the morning. I will give you the loan of my carriage if that is what you wish, my dear. But I will not stand by and have your reputation ruined by a fortune hunter." He put a reassuring hand over hers to silence her rebuttal. "Being thought eccentric because you teach cits is one thing. Earning the reputation of a lightskirt I cannot allow."

"Harry! It was never like that! And I have no intention . . ."

"It doesn't require your intention to commit mayhem for it to occur," said her knowing brother. He rose, leaving her to her own troubled thoughts. At the door, he added, "Whatever happened to that skinny little girl whom our dear father paralyzed with fear about fortune hunters? The one who was too shy to enjoy her first ball, who believed all men only wanted her inheritance, not her? You've changed, Hetty."

He closed the door behind him, leaving Hetty to ponder his last cryptic remark.

Suddenly, the door opened, and her twin reappeared.

Grinning like a schoolboy, he said, "I meant for the better, of course."

She stuck out her tongue and gave a feeble laugh.

From all outward appearances, Jared was perfectly content with his new position in life. He attended any entertainment which appealed to him, boxed at Jackson's Salon, shot at Manton's Gallery, even became a regular at White's. All the while, however, he made certain he was never in a vulnerable position. Though he continued to ride in the park, he varied his schedule and always took a groom along to help exercise another horse.

The blooming friendship between him and his cousin Casper cooled considerably, although Jared never accused him of the ambush in the park. In truth, he doubted Casper had the nerve to shoot anyone.

Without Casper, however, he was finding his new position very solitary. People called at his town house, but not the one he wanted to see—Hetty. One morning, however, his melancholy was interrupted by a welcome face.

"Norton!" Jared rose and pumped his solicitor's hand as if he were a long-lost friend. Looking past his friend to the butler, he said, "Martin, bring us something to eat and drink. I'm suddenly famished."

"My lord, thank you," squeaked the little man, "but I have come on business."

"Yes? Well, come and sit down. If you have brought me bad news and I am ruined, take comfort in the fact I am still better off now than when you found me," teased Jared.

"No, no, my lord, I assure you it is nothing of the sort. As a matter of fact, it is more a matter of my business than yours."

Jared sat forward, listening attentively. "I'll do anything I can to help, Tobias."

The use of his Christian name made Norton smile. No matter what happened, the marquess Winter would always defy protocol and address his employee as a friend.

"I would like to buy the house on South Audley, my lord."

"You needn't buy it. I will give it to you," said Jared. "After all you have done for me, it's probably due to you."

"Not at all, my lord. I am well paid for my position."

"Then I will sell it to you for one pound sterling."

"No, no, my lord. I could not allow you to be swindled in such a matter. Remember, I handle your finances also."

"Then what can I do?"

"It is just that Angel, Mrs. Grant, really likes living there. I . . . that is, we . . ."

"Well, I'll be! You're going to marry the . . ." Jared pulled up short. Instead of completing his thought, he began to pump Norton's hand. "Congratulations! She's a wonderful girl!"

Sobering, Norton pulled his hand free and said, "I know all about Angel's past, my lord. You mustn't think she tried to deceive me. I know I am not the only man in her life. But whatever she *was,* she will be my wife."

"I know, Tobias. And I know she will make you happy."

"I only hope I can measure up." He flushed an uncomfortable shade of red.

"I'd say you can measure up to anyone, Tobias. And I'll tell you what I want to do. There's this fellow I know who's been a real friend to me. He's getting married, and I want to give him a decent sort of wedding present. He's marrying an old friend of mine, too, so it's important that I give them something special, like a house. Do you know of one I own that might be suitable?" asked Jared, his blue eyes twinkling in a manner almost forgotten in the past weeks.

"I believe there is a house," said Norton, shaking Jared's hand, "a most suitable one."

When Hetty reached London, she resisted the temptation to go directly to the house on South Audley Street. First of all, she was unsure if Jared still resided there. Second, she was very much afraid he did.

Sanders, who had been enjoying a respite while in the country, was quite happy to feel useful to his mistress again. Molly, however, who had family at Bosworth, grumbled under her breath as she unpacked Hetty's things.

"Could have sent a note to that Mr. Norton," she said, a little too loudly.

"Yes, I could have, but I would never have known if he had taken it seriously and warned Lord Winter.

And then how would I feel if someone killed him?" said Hetty tartly, her voice trembling only slightly at the thought of Jared's murder.

"Beg pardon, my lady," said Molly, whose years of loyal service helped her hear the tremor in her mistress's voice. She added contritely, "You must forgive an old woman."

"It's all right, Molly. I forgive you. I know you miss your family. You know, you could return to Bosworth if you wanted. I could find someone . . ."

"As if I would leave my lamb to the mercies of some stranger!" said the indignant maid. "Why, I'd as lief abandon a newborn babe, I would."

Smiling, Hetty left the room, content to know she had given Molly's grumbling a new turn.

She made her way through the gardens to the tiny stables, hoping to find Ned. He came out of the garden shed bearing a basket of bulbs.

"What are you planting, Ned?" she inquired.

"I was just separating some more of them jonquils you set such store by, miss. They'll be shooting up before we know it."

"Yes, spring is just around the corner," said Hetty, following the gardener to the bed he was planting.

"When will old Daisy be coming back to us?" he asked.

"His grace has persuaded me to leave Daisy at Bosworth, Ned," said Hetty.

"I suppose that's best for the old girl, but I'll miss her, I will."

"Me, too. But we will have another one. I picked

out a sweet mare from my brother's stable. She's only eight years old, almost a baby," said Hetty, grinning.

"Good for you!" he said. "I'll make sure the stall is clean and dry for her, miss."

"Thank you." She tried to think how to phrase her next question. Finally, she asked, "Tell me, Ned, was there any excitement around the house while I was gone?"

"No, miss. Nothing comes to mind."

"Any visitors?" she probed, thinking surely Mr. Norton had tried to contact her.

"No, miss. Not in the past few weeks," he said, ceasing his labors and looking thoughtful. "Now the day you left, there was quite a to-do. I shouldn't have opened th' door at all, I suppose. I had already removed the knocker, you see."

In breathless tones, Hetty said, "Someone came by?"

"Yes, miss, a foreign fellow and a fidgety little man. Th' big one, he grabbed me by the collar and nearly shook my teeth out of my head!"

"Oh, Ned, I am sorry," said Hetty, a tremor of excitement running through her. Only Jared would have acted so impulsively. "Then what?"

"He wanted to know where you had gone, what your family name was, but I wouldn't tell him!" said Ned proudly. "I figured if you had wanted him t' know, you would have told him yourself!"

Hetty smiled, but her heart was near to breaking. He had come for her. Controlling her ricocheting emotions, she said, "Thank you, Ned. You did well. Anyone else?"

"Just yesterday, a tall, heavyset man. But I sent him about his business, too."

"Good. Thank you," she said, forcing a weak smile.

Hetty turned back to the house, strolling listlessly through the bare garden, thinking how fitting it was the day should be so gloomy. She paused, frowning.

Retracing her steps, Hetty asked quickly, "Ned, was there anyone else with them, the foreigner and the fidgety man? A woman, perhaps?"

He scratched his head, looking thoughtful for a moment before saying slowly, "Nobody, miss, 'cept the two gentry morts."

"Thank you, Ned." Hetty returned to the house with alacrity. At least *that woman* had not been with Jared!

She hurried into the salon, glanced at her reflection in the mirror, and nodded. She would do. The clock began to chime four o'clock. Time enough for a quick drive.

"Sanders, send for a hackney cab, please. I have an errand to perform," she said.

At a snail's pace, the butler hurried to do her bidding. For the first time, Hetty wished she had a younger servant. Things had gone much more smoothly at Jared's house, where the footman had been present to carry out Sanders's orders.

Hetty tripped up the steps to her room to fetch her cloak. Molly frowned as she donned the black garment and a matching bonnet.

"It's too late for the shops, my lady," she said.

"I'm not going to the shops, Molly," said Hetty, knowing her face was flushed with excitement and her eyes were sparkling. "Do not scold, Molly, or I won't let you come with me!"

The maid's natural retort was cut short as she went to get her own hat and coat.

A misty rain was falling by the time the driver pulled up across the street from the house on South Audley.

"Anything else, ma'am?" said the driver.

"Just stay right here while I get my bearings," she said, her eyes peering through the gloom to the familiar house.

Just then the door opened, and Jared appeared on the threshold. Hetty watched in dismay as two slender, feminine arms crept around his neck in a spirited hug. He started down the steps, waving to the woman in the doorway, Angel Grant. Molly gasped, and Hetty turned away, bowing her head to avoid possible detection.

When Jared had driven away, Hetty said miserably, "Take me back to Cavendish Square, driver."

Molly patted her mistress's hand but wisely remained silent.

Hetty resisted the inclination to cry. There was no reason to, really. It was not as if she had expected to return to London and find Jared pining for her, waiting with open arms. She had only wanted to warn him to beware his cousins. She ignored the inner voice that mocked her.

Truly, she told herself, there had never been any promises, any understanding between them.

And that was the trouble, she thought miserably.

There had never been *anything* between them. How she wished there had been.

At least then, she would have some memories.

Nine

In secret we met—
In silence I grieve,
That thy heart could forget,
Thy spirit deceive.

—Lord Byron

"What the devil do you mean, you haven't been able to find out anything about her? I thought you were supposed to be the best in the world!" Jared raged at his target, the Bow Street Runner named Taggert.

"Best there is, my lord," said the runner, unruffled by his employer's outburst. "The thing is, it's harder t' find someone if they don't want t' be found. Could be, my lord, this lady doesn't want you to find *'er.*"

The muscle twitching in Jared's jaw looked ready to spring forth, but he held his tongue.

"I went back t' that house you told me about on Cavendish Square again yesterday. There was only that gardener there. No sign anyone else has been there, and he's still not talking. I think it's safe t' say the lady's not in London."

"And do you not look for people outside of London?" came the question with deadly calm.

"O' course, milord. But that takes time, an' I've got t' have something to go on."

"And how are you going to find something to 'go on' when you can't even pry a bloody name out of a gardener?" shouted Jared.

"I want t' talk t' that Norton fellow again. You won't talk to the gentry for fear o' ruining the lady's reputation. Maybe this solicitor fellow will remember some clue as to the lady's relatives."

Jared sat down at his desk and scribbled the address. "Here! Go and see Norton. I don't understand how he can possibly help you, but go see him anyway. I've asked and asked, but he says the man who told him about Miss Thompson is completely ignorant of her family name."

The runner pocketed the piece of paper and nodded, sauntering from the room.

"At least you'll be out of my sight!" muttered Jared.

"My lord, Mr. Golightly to see you," said his efficient butler.

"Send him in."

"Shall I serve luncheon?"

"Why not? At least somebody will be doing something," he said sourly.

"Cousin! How nice to see you looking so . . . fit." Casper wished with every word he had chosen another time to visit his new cousin, who appeared ready to murder someone . . . anyone! Flipping up the tails to his new coat so they wouldn't wrinkle, he sat down gingerly on the nearest chair.

"Have a seat, Casper," said Jared, studying his cousin's newest sartorial effort with derision.

Casper appeared disconcerted, gave a nervous giggle, and forged ahead. "I came by to see if you are going to be using your box at the theater tonight. My mother wants . . ." Jared's glare unnerved him so, he rose and said apologetically, "But I see this was a bad time to call. I'll come back later."

Jared shook his head and sat up straight. His attempt to smile was not wholly successful, but he said in a more friendly tone, "Nonsense, Casper. Sit down. If your mother wishes to use my box, she is welcome to it. I was not planning to attend the theater tonight."

"Mother will be so pleased," said the dutiful son, relieved to know he would be relaying welcome news to his parent. Then he recalled his cousin's mood, and asked sympathetically, "But, Jared, whatever is the matter? Is there something wrong? Can I help?"

Jared's laugh held only self-recrimination. "Nothing, Cousin, unless you can produce the elusive woman I mean to marry."

"Marry!" chirped Casper, his own manner becoming harried. Whatever would his mother say when she found out Jared planned to wed? She would be beside herself, and she would take it out on him! Somehow, she would make it his fault.

Casper laughed nervously. "But, Jared, a fellow has to find his own wife. I don't suppose anyone can help you do that!"

"No, probably not," Jared said glumly, causing his cousin to brighten.

A footman entered with the tray of food, and Jared invited his cousin to stay and join him.

Rising again, Casper said, "No, Jared, I think not. I must hurry home and tell Mother she can go to the theater as planned. Thank you."

Jared waved his cousin away, looked at the food, and rose, leaving the room also. He ordered a horse saddled and climbed the stairs to get his heavy cloak, for the day had turned raw.

At home in New Orleans, March was wet, but not usually cold like this. Jared thought he might have better off if he had stayed there.

"Hetty, Harry and I really wish you would come to stay with us at Bosworth House for the Season. You do not have any students at the moment," said Amy, her overly perceptive sister-in-law, "so there is nothing keeping you here."

"Really, Amy, I no longer fit in with the Polite World." Hetty poured a cup of tea and handed it to Amy.

They sat in the front salon of the house in Cavendish Square only one week after Hetty's return to London. Her brother, she knew, had quickly altered his plans and removed to the town house off Grosvenor Square so he could watch over her. She didn't care as long as he left her alone. The last thing she wanted was to be eternally underfoot in Amy's house.

"What nonsense!" said Amy. "You are the sister to a duke. Besides, Perry Bigglesby told Harry you promised to help find him a wife this Season."

"I thought he was to wed the squire's niece, that Catherine Tilbury," Hetty said.

"That's right! You left before that particular disaster was played out!" Amy lowered her voice and glanced toward the salon door, as if Sanders's ears were keen enough to hear through it.

"What happened? Do not tell me she turned Perry down!"

"No, no, nothing of the sort! Perry discovered, quite by accident, that she drank!"

"That pretty little girl?" Hetty asked, astounded.

"Indeed! He called on her the day after our dinner party. I believe he was going there for the express purpose of proposing. Anyway, she was in the squire's salon, singing a song at the pianoforte, a glass of port or something at her elbow. He thought nothing of it until she spoke. It was then he realized she was intoxicated in the middle of the afternoon! Can you imagine?"

"Poor Perry," said Hetty. "Was he very upset?"

"I don't think so. He appeared fine that evening at supper. It was just the three of us, and he admitted he felt quite lucky to have discovered the truth before marrying her."

"Then he has come to London to find a wife?"

"Yes, and he said you promised to help!"

Hetty grinned ruefully. "So I did, and I accused him at the time of conspiring with you and Harry against me."

"Then you will come and stay with us?" asked Amy.

"No, but I will attend a few of the entertainments, if you think anyone will invite me. I haven't minded in the least being forgotten for the past five years, but I do hope I won't receive the cut direct. That would be too lowering," said Hetty.

Her sister-in-law squared her shoulders, raised her chin, and looked down her nose at Hetty, intoning regally, "Lady Henrietta, sister of the Duke of Bosworth, receiving the cut direct? Never, my dear! Oh, we shall have such fun! It is so much more pleasant when one is settled, you'll find. You will actually be able to enjoy yourself!"

When Amy had departed, Hetty wandered around the neat room. Since returning to London the week before, she had suffered from an intense restlessness. If she were completely truthful with herself, she would have admitted the restlessness had appeared only after seeing Jared in the arms of Angel Grant.

She had called at the newspaper office to place an advertisement for some new pupils, but the idea simply didn't appeal to her, and she had left without doing so. When she sat down to play her lyre, or to finish the one she was working on, her mind wandered, and she accomplished nothing.

Now she had promised to attend some of the Season's functions, she knew she should go through her wardrobe with Molly, visit the dressmaker, purchase new bonnets, new gloves, and so on, but the thought of bestirring herself for such activities was unbearable.

Hetty strolled to the window, staring outside but not taking in the scene. She shook her head in frustration. If only she had never met Jared, Lord Winter!

Hetty focused on a man who was lingering across the street, leaning against the house opposite hers. He was studying his shoes, or else he was dozing standing up. It was as if he felt her gaze, for he looked up sharply, meeting her eyes, then pushed away from the house and walked hurriedly away.

Hetty tried to shake off the disquiet she felt, but it was impossible. There could be no reason for anyone to watch her house, but she had not been mistaken.

She moved to the escritoire and composed two brief notes. Stepping into the front hall, she said, "Sanders, would you have Ned take this to Bow Street? I hope to have an answer to it this afternoon, possibly even a caller. And have the new footman carry this one to my brother."

"Yes, miss," said the butler.

"And, Sanders, I know I needn't warn you to keep this to yourself."

"Of course not, miss!"

She turned to retrace her steps, thought better of it, and said, "One more thing, Sanders. My sister-in-law insists I accompany her to numerous entertainments during the coming Season. Knowing the Polite World, this may entail visitors to Cavendish Square."

"Undoubtedly," said the butler.

"Therefore, I think it would be better if the staff began calling me by my proper title again."

"Very good, Lady Henrietta."

The butler toddled away, and Hetty sighed. How she hated that name. But would she shock the *ton* if she insisted everyone call her Lady Hetty? It was terribly informal and suited her so much better, but her teachers at the seminary for young ladies had refused to allow her to use it. They had insisted on calling her Lady Henrietta, and so would the *ton*.

Hetty sighed. Now she recalled why she had found being a member of the Polite World so burdensome!

"I don't wish you to think I am suffering from paranoia, Mr. Arnold, but it was very frightening when I realized that man was watching my house."

"Is there anything unusual about this house, Lady Henrietta?" asked the man, jotting down notes in a small notebook. He licked the end of his pencil and waited, poised for her next words.

"Nothing, and I have few valuables. I wondered if my brother had possibly sent a man to watch over me."

"And would there be some reason for that?"

"No, but he is rather protective. When my brother received my note he came right over, but he denied having the house watched."

"Hmm." The man frowned and pursed his lips as he pondered her problem. "And you say you haven't seen the man since then?"

"No, I haven't seen him."

"I'll tell you what, my lady. I'll just stay close tonight and keep an eye on things."

"Would you like me to have a bed made up?" asked Hetty.

"No, no, I won't be sleeping, my lady. That would defeat my purposes, wouldn't it?"

"Since I am not acquainted with the manner in which your office operates, Mr. Arnold, I have no idea," Hetty said. How she despised condescending men.

"Of course not, my lady." The Bow Street Runner shifted uncomfortably under her raised brow. "I'll just be around the outside of the house. Please warn your people not to take a shot at me!"

"I will tell my man Ned. He is the only one you need worry about. Sanders never goes outside, but I will tell him and he will make certain the rest of the staff remains inside."

"Very good, then. I'll be going now."

When she was alone again, Hetty walked to the window, peering into the gathering darkness. She realized suddenly that she was standing in the light, easily visible from the street. Hastily, she pulled the curtain closed.

Jared had seldom played cards for pleasure. Now that he no longer needed to play and win for the money, he found little pleasure in it. Still, when the Duke of Bosworth sought him out at White's for a hand of piquet, he thought it wise to accept.

"You're a very shrewd player, Lord Winter," said the duke after an hour of play as he tallied up the scores.

"I do my best," said Jared. "If I was supposed to let you win, your being a duke and all, you'll have to forgive me. I haven't quite got the hang of this rank and title business."

Harry laughed. "No, no, you can beat me as badly as you wish. I was going to say as badly as I allow, but that is only too true. I am not the best card player in the world, I know. They tell me I have too honest a face."

"Too open," Jared agreed, "but I think there is a hidden talent there."

"You're too kind." Harry lowered his eyes to shuffle the cards. The clock chimed eleven. He wondered how Hetty was doing. Was she still distressed about that strange man? Somehow, he felt sure the marquess Winter was at the bottom of it. He hoped Perry was still keeping an eye on her house.

Looking up, he asked, "Tell me, Winter, are you married?"

"No, never have been. You?"

Harry grinned, feeling an absurd flood of relief to learn the marquess had not been wed when he and Hetty were . . . well, thought Harry, whatever it was they were doing together.

Harry responded casually, "Hmm, to a lovely girl. We have four children, too."

"You don't seem old enough." Jared studied the cards dealt to him.

"I'm not," laughed Harry. "We have two sets of twins, two boys and two girls. I'm a twin myself," he added, watching his opponent closely for some sign of recognition, remembrance, something. Of course, he had no way of knowing if Hetty had mentioned being a twin.

A footman approached them with a silver tray and extended it to Jared. He took the envelope and opened it, scanning the contents quickly.

"If you'll excuse me, Bosworth, something of great

importance has just come to my attention. I really must be going." Jared rose as he spoke.

"Nothing bad, I hope," said the duke.

"No, nothing like that. Something quite good, as a matter of fact. Good night!" said Jared, hurrying to the door of the club.

Harry rose also, his mission for the night completed. He took a sedan chair home and entered the elegant town house just off Grosvenor Square, grinning at the butler as he flipped his hat off his head, down his arm, and into the servant's waiting hands. Then, at a most unstately pace, he climbed the stairs two at a time, whistling loudly.

"Harry, shh! You'll wake the children!" said his wife, opening her arms to embrace him.

"They're all the way upstairs!" He kissed her soundly and led her back into their apartments.

"You are certainly in a better frame of mind than you were this afternoon," commented the duchess, sitting on his lap, his arms holding her firmly in place.

"You could say that. I didn't wish to worry you, my dear, but after speaking to Hetty about that man watching her house, I was rather shaken. I immediately thought of Winter."

"Why? From what Hetty said about him, and I grant you she was rather vague, they were the best of friends." His wife smoothed the downy curls away from his forehead.

"I know, but you know Hetty, taking in every stray she finds. Why, her entire household consists of animals and servants she's rescued. Where men are concerned, she is an innocent. And here's this fellow, new to London, unsure of our ways, just the sort of project for my sister."

"Hetty is no fool, Harry," said Amy.

"No, she isn't. But how can I trust her judgment on men? She has so little experience," he said, nuzzling his wife's neck.

"I didn't think of that." Amy suddenly pushed away from Harry, saying, "What does all this have to do with the man in the street?"

"I couldn't help but wonder, if this fellow—Winter, I mean—were an out-and-out rogue, would she be able to tell? What if he had formed some unnatural attachment to her?"

The duchess rose and pulled him to his feet. "Well, what if he did?" she asked in alarm.

"Don't worry, my dear, that's why I sought him out at the club. Over a glass or two, a hand or two of cards, one can take the measure of a man."

"And you think he is a decent sort?" she asked anxiously.

"Yes, very decent. I mean, he beat me at cards handily, but that is no reason to suspect him of being deranged."

"Deranged? Oh, Harry, now I am worried! What if he sent that man to watch our Hetty? What if he means to kidnap her? Or . . . or worse!"

"You've been reading too many novels!" The duke laughed and put his arms around his wife again. "Besides, Perry is watching the house."

"All night? No, Harry, it's just . . . I have the most lowering suspicion that all is not as it should be with

Hetty. Don't you feel it?" she demanded, taking his hands in hers.

His wife's anxiety was contagious, and Harry took a step away, shaking his head. "We're just overreacting, Amy. Besides, Hetty can take care of herself. She was expecting a Bow Street Runner any minute when I left her this afternoon."

"A Bow Street Runner! She must be frightened to death!" exclaimed the duchess. "If you're not going over there to be with her, then I am!"

"No, no, you should stay here, my dear," said the duke. "I'll go. I couldn't sleep now, anyway." He crossed the room to a locked cabinet and removed a carved wooden box.

The duchess gasped, saying, "Surely you won't need a pistol."

"I want to be prepared," came his grim reply. "I'll not be home until daylight, my dear."

"And I'll not sleep until you are," she whispered, returning his quick embrace. "Be careful, love."

"Taggert, are you sure?" whispered Jared. "How did your man describe the woman he saw today?"

The runner responded in gruffly hushed tones, "Waller said th' woman was obviously quality, a matron of some years."

Jared expelled a frustrated sigh. "How many years? Thirty? Forty? Sixty?"

"He didn't say exactly. He said she had dark hair."

"Taggert, I don't know what I'm paying you for! Your cohort comes back with little more than the information that the house is now occupied!" Jared's voice rose as he spoke, leaving his listener in the uncomfortable position of having to shush a marquess.

Deciding to lead by example, Taggert whispered, "But it was the same man, milord. That Ned person is still there. Stands to reason it's the same female as what yer lookin' for."

"And am I supposed to call at the door on that slim line of reasoning?"

"No, milord. As I told you, I can get in through the garden gate and take a look in th' window."

"And do what? Come back and tell me the woman is a matron somewhere between twenty and one hundred?" Jared glared at the patient runner, knowing he was being unreasonable, but not caring. If this man had raised his hopes only to have them dashed, Jared would very probably strangle him!

"Then you can go, milord. I'll keep watch."

Jared turned this idea over in his mind for only a few seconds before saying, "Very well. At least I will be doing something. And, Taggert . . ."

"Yes, milord?"

"Sorry about losing my temper."

Taggert looked shocked at this apology and hastily said, "No need for apologies, milord. I'm just doin' my job best I can."

When they arrived in the alley behind Hetty's house, Jared asked, "Can you make a bird call to warn me if you see anything?"

"Who, who," said the man in his low, gravelly voice.

Jared grinned, shaking his head. "Just call out," he

said, opening the squeaky garden gate and stepping inside.

Hetty reached for the candle stand on the table by her bed, thought better of it, and moved silently to the door of her bedchamber. She made her way to her sitting room, planning to play her lyre to calm her frazzled nerves. She opened the armoire before she recalled she had taken it downstairs to the study the day before.

Again, she thought of lighting the candles, but she didn't wish to alarm the Bow Street Runner lurking somewhere outside the house. Putting on her old wrapper, she made her way without mishap through the dark house to the study. Heavy curtains drawn across the French doors that overlooked the garden left the room in total obscurity.

Feeling her way along the wall to the doors, Hetty pulled the heavy draperies to one side. With her back to the glass doors, she allowed her eyes to adjust for a moment and surveyed the room for her lyre.

The maid must have moved it, she thought, looking at the chair where she had sat to play the instrument. She crossed to the other side of the double doors, pulling the draperies as she went to allow more moonlight inside.

Suddenly, Hetty froze, her heart pounding in her breast. A quiet whine made her shoulders sag with relief.

"Penny," she whispered, "who let you outside at this time of night?" She turned the latch on the door and opened it just enough to allow the little hound inside. Fastening the lock, she stooped down to pet the dancing dog.

"Come on," Hetty said, somehow feeling infinitely more secure with her small friend by her side. She collected the lyre from the bookshelf where the maid had left it and started for the door. At the foot of the stairs, Penny started to whine, refusing to follow.

"What now?" The dog stood on its hind legs and whirled around, whimpering. "Shh, all right. We'll see what we can find in the kitchen. But no more begging," she admonished.

Hetty, who had eaten almost nothing since morning, found a cold meat pasty in the larder to share with her dog. She hesitated, knowing if she returned to her room, her playing would wake Molly. The study, which was well-insulated by its many bookshelves, would be the best place. Accordingly, she led the way back to the study.

"Here you go," she said, breaking off a portion and placing it on a saucer for the dog before tasting some herself. Tasting the food awakened her senses, and Hetty shivered. The fire had burned itself out, but with some coaxing, a tiny flame sprang forth. Hetty added some kindling and watched the light grow.

Full and warm, she picked up her lyre and began to strum, her unsteady voice singing the melody.

> *"The king sits in Dumferling toune,*
> *Drinking the blude-reid wine:*
> *O whar will I get . . ."*

Penny's head jerked up, and she growled.

The light of the moon faded as a cloud passed overhead. Hetty froze, incapable of speech or movement as someone scratched at the glass of the French doors. Slinking behind her mistress, Penny continued to growl.

Did I lock it? thought Hetty, horrified, as the latch began to move.

In a flash, she ran to the door, her hand feeling for the lock. With a triumphant twist, she relaxed, only to realize an instant later she had released it instead, unwittingly allowing entry to the shadowy figure outside.

Strong hands grasped her wrists.

"Hetty!"

"Hetty!"

"Milady!"

"Lady Henrietta!"

"Milord!"

"Harry!"

"Perry?"

The names competed from faraway, drowned out by the ringing in her ears as she tottered on the edge of unconsciousness. Then one voice superseded all the others, and she looked up, searching for its owner amid the chaos surrounding her.

"Jared!" she whispered, her voice too low for anyone to hear. A wave of relief washed over her.

Then she focused on the crowd that had somehow gathered in her garden—all flailing legs, arms, hoes, pistols—and Penny's frenzied yapping.

"Hellfire and damnation!" shouted Jared, losing all pretense of gentility. "Get your bloody hands off me!"

"Aha! So it was you, Winter!" yelled Harry.

"I've got him now, mistress!" shouted Ned.

Other voices, strange voices, began to untangle themselves from the melee.

"Hands up!" ordered Hetty's Bow Street Runner. Then, "That you, Taggert? Waller?"

"Arnold? What the devil are you doing here?"

"Harry? What the deuce you doing here? I thought I was supposed to take the first watch!" burst out Perry Bigglesby.

Shaking her head, Hetty glared at the lot of them. Gathering her old wrapper around her nightgown, she donned her best schoolmistress manner and said crisply, "When you have finished making fools of yourselves, gentlemen, I want you, all of you, to get out of my garden. For that matter, get out of my life!"

With that, she shut the French doors, turned the lock, and pulled the heavy draperies closed.

Penny, who was still barking, was silenced with a stern, "No!"

Passing silently past Sanders in his nightcap, the cook with her rolling pin, the maid, the new footman, and the faithful Molly, Hetty kept her head high. She climbed the stairs to her room, allowed the cowed hound inside, and shut and locked the door.

Hetty got into bed, her anger softening as she listened to the muffled conversation beneath her window. Her lips curved into a slow smile, and a reticent, oft-quashed voice sang:

He came looking for me!

Ten

As fair art thou, my bonnie lass
So deep in luve am I,
And I will luve thee still, my dear,
Till a' the seas gang dry.
                                    —*Robert Burns*

Jared untangled himself from his captors. Arnold, Hetty's runner, seemed reluctant to let go of the marquess's collar and only did so when he had been dragged two or three paces.

"Do you have any idea who I am?" asked Jared, looking down at the other man, his nostrils flared, his temper in shreds, and his patience extinct.

"Let him be," advised Taggert.

"But this here must be the man my lady saw watching 'er 'ouse." Arnold loosened his grip slowly.

"You've got it all wrong, Arnold," said Taggert, rising from his position and brushing off his coat. "That was Waller here. I set him t' watching out for the lady's return."

Ignoring the runners, Jared turned curious eyes on

his recent piquet challenger. "Bosworth, what the deuce are you doing here?"

"I could ask you the same thing, Winter," Harry said, taking his handkerchief from a torn pocket and gingerly dabbing at his swollen, bloody lip. "Might be more to the point, too." He winced as he touched his forehead.

"And who the devil are you?" Jared demanded, looking the tall Mr. Bigglesby in the eye.

"I've got more right to be here than you," declared Perry slowly.

"He's with me," said Harry. "Why don't you go home, Perry?"

"Yes, do go home, Perry," mocked Jared, his comment causing the peaceful Mr. Bigglesby to close his fists.

" 'Ere now, all o' you, out you go, just like milady said," decreed Ned, still wielding his hoe. "Go on!"

Perry trudged toward the garden gate, but Jared looked ready for another set-to.

Harry chuckled and said, "Come along, Winter. We can't talk here. Where are you staying?"

"My town house," replied Jared, allowing the duke to usher him through the garden.

They were followed by the three runners, still exchanging their tales of inanity. Bringing up the rear was Ned, his hoe aimed and ready if any of them should make a break for the house.

"Your place is closer. I hope you have had time to stock the cellar." Harry clapped the wary marquess on the back and guided him along the back alley toward the street.

* * *

By unspoken agreement, the two men made the short trek in silence. Jared's starchy butler opened the front door and lost only a second's dignity as he stared at the torn and tattered peers.

"Come in, your grace, my lord," he sputtered.

"Is the fire made up in the library, Martin?"

"Indeed, yes, my lord."

"Good. Andy could you see if something in the way of food is available?"

"Very good, my lord. Shall I serve your drinks first?"

"No, I can manage that," said Jared dryly, crossing the thickly carpeted room to a sideboard with full decanters and clean glasses.

"What can I get for you, your grace?" he asked.

"I'll have whatever you do, Winter. As long as it's strong, it will be fine with me. Might I have one of your people take a note to my wife to let her know everything has turned out all right? I know she will not be able to sleep until she hears the outcome."

"Of course. There's the bellpull." Jared indicated the long piece of tapestry hanging beside the fireplace. "You'll find pen and paper on the desk."

When Harry had taken care of his business, he joined Jared by the fire, taking a jade-colored chair made of the softest leather. Jared lounged on the sofa, studying his guest with open curiosity.

"Shall I begin first?" asked Harry, giving his host his good-natured grin.

"Might as well, since I have nothing to say." Jared took a sip of the whiskey he favored.

Harry followed suit, recoiling with a grimace as the liquor touched his cut lip. He set the glass on the table and leaned forward.

"Hetty is my sister, my twin sister," he said simply.

Jared's deadpan expression gave nothing away. "So?"

"No, Winter, that's not how it works. I have just given you a vital piece of information. Now it is your turn."

"I'm afraid I can't help you, old boy," Jared said in his best English accent, his calm maddening.

Harry jumped to his feet, glaring at Jared, who continued to sip from his glass. Though he maintained his air of detachment, Jared's mind was working quickly.

If what Bosworth says is true—and he has no reason to lie—it follows he knows about the time Hetty and I spent together. He probably wants to call me out. Dueling with Hetty's brother, her twin brother, is the last thing I want to do, he thought. *However, Hetty might not have told her brother. If not, I certainly don't want to.*

Wrestling with this dilemma, Jared missed Harry's question and unintentionally angered his guest even more. Harry reached for Jared's collar, but his hands were caught in an iron grip and never touched the garment. Jared jumped to his feet, towering over Harry. He released Bosworth's wrists and braced himself, knowing his opponent planned to throw his best punch.

The door to the library opened. A footman entered, followed by Jared's butler, who nervously directed the placement of the tray.

"Will there be . . ."

"Get out," said Jared, not daring to take his eyes off Harry.

"Very good, my lord." The butler hurried away, the interested footman following reluctantly.

With a crooked smile, Jared suggested, "Shall we eat before we fight? It's been a devilishly long day, and I am starving." Harry nodded, and they sat down again.

Jared speared a slab of ham, packed it in between some bread, and took a huge bite. Harry began to eat, also, and soon the two men were allied in action, if not emotion.

Jared washed the food down with the remainder of his whiskey. Harry turned to ale, finding the taste much more to his liking. The swelling of his lip had receded, and it no longer burned to the touch.

Leaning back against the soft cushions, Jared sighed in contentment, his physical needs met. Harry was not so easily restored, and watched his host warily.

"Look, Bosworth, it will do us no good to go at it again," said Jared. "Tell me what you know, and I'll fill in the gaps."

"I know my sister was a fool to move into a house with a strange man, no matter how dire his need for tutoring might be, but Hetty was ever the one to take in strays."

Jared acknowledged the insult with a nod, but didn't speak.

Harry continued, "I know something happened that drove her away, more upset than I have seen her since our father died. Yet, despite whatever this scoundrel did to her, she returned to London for the express purpose of warning him of the danger she fancied he was in."

Jared scratched his chin thoughtfully, then said, "You know more than I do, I think. At least you know more about what has happened recently. Hetty, er, Miss Thompson . . . whatever you think I should call her . . . she and I became very close. And you can quit reaching for that sword you're not wearing, Bosworth. No one despises knowing she has been hurt more than I do. I would cut off my right arm if . . ."

"I had other things in mind," Harry said grimly.

"Look, you're angry. You want to protect your sister, but you've got to trust her, and that means trusting me."

"Not my first choice there, either," murmured Harry.

"No, I suppose it's not. So what are you going to do?"

"I think I shall take Hetty and my wife and return to Bosworth."

"Won't do you any good now," said Jared, his blue eyes as cold as ice. "Now that I know her name, I'll follow her."

"And when you do, Winter, what then?"

"I don't think I can tell you, Bosworth. I'll have to ask Hetty how this is going to end. It's up to her."

Harry rose, knowing he was not physically able to

force Jared to leave Hetty alone. Furthermore, he wasn't certain he should.

"Just tell me two things, Winter."

"If I can."

"I asked you this at the club, but I want the truth now. Are you already married?"

"No," said Jared, grinning for the first time at the obstinate duke.

Harry grunted, satisfied with this response. Abruptly he added, "Do you love my sister?"

Jared's grin softened, and he said, "I'm afraid I do."

The clock chimed three as Jared wearily climbed the stairs to his bed. He stripped down to his unmentionables and stretched, his arms high above his head. A roaring fire burned in the grate, although the evening was rather mild.

"May I get you anything, my lord?" said Gibbons, covering his yawn as he entered the room.

"What are you doing up? Go back to bed."

"If you insist, my lord," said the valet, gathering the soiled clothes Jared had draped over the bedpost. "Shall I crack the window? I know you like a little fresh air at night."

"Yes, thank you." Jared bent over to remove his shoes.

Gibbons moved to the window and opened it a few inches. There was a loud pop, and the valet screamed, pitching forward onto the carpet. Jared rushed to his side.

"What is it, man?" when he grabbed the valet by

the shoulders, his hand came away warm and sticky. "My God, you've been shot!"

"Shot?" murmured the valet. He fainted and fell back on the carpet.

The sound of running feet alerted Jared to the servants about to descend on them. He loosened Gibbons's collar and probed the wounded area. The valet groaned and his eyes fluttered open.

"What was that, my lord?" exclaimed Martin, throwing open the door and stepping inside. He turned just in time to catch one of the maids as she swooned. Throwing the girl to a footman, he hurried to his master's side.

"He's been shot, but I think it went straight through," said Jared. "I don't feel the slug. Get me some whiskey to clean it and lots of clean cloths. He's bleeding like the devil."

No one moved.

"Don't just stand there gawking! Do as I say!" roared the marquess.

The footman handed the limp maid to the next, saying he would fetch the surgeon. Martin sent the housekeeper for the required medicaments.

Then, leaning over the marquess's shoulder, Martin asked bluntly, "Shall I send for that runner, my lord?"

Their eyes met over the wounded valet, and Jared nodded, his own visage forbidding.

Jared's meeting with Taggert was another exercise in frustration. Without any real proof, they couldn't very well arrest Casper Golightly, which left Jared looking over his shoulder every time he stepped out of the house—not to mention his fears for Hetty.

"I really want to put an end to this whole ugly mess, Taggert. I'm hoping to get married, and I don't want to place my wife in danger."

"I understand," said the runner.

"I just can't believe that milquetoast would do it." Jared rose and stretched his aching muscles. He had dozed only fitfully since Gibbons had been shot.

"Tell me, did Mr. Golightly know about your plans to marry? If he did, that could make him desperate, especially if he's up to his ears in debt."

"I did mention it, but that was before . . . Taggert, what will happen if we can prove my cousin is behind these attempts on my life?" he asked.

"That is largely up to you, milord. He might be hanged or transported."

"Look into his finances," Jared said. "I want to know how deep in debt he is."

"Very good, milord."

"I'm going to see what kind of horses he has in his stable." Jared closed his eyes briefly, knowing rest was out of the question until he had done this last thing.

Jared rode past the small house Casper and his mother shared and entered the narrow alley in the back. The fence was wrought iron, the garden green and tidy. There was no stable, and Jared was nonplussed. *Surely,* he thought, *Casper keeps horses and a carriage.*

Returning to the front of the house, Jared lifted the knocker. A butler in modest livery opened the door and accepted his card, then ushered Jared into a small, dark library where Casper sat at a table, intently studying a jigsaw puzzle.

Casper appeared gratified by his cousin's unexpected visit. "By jingo, this is a pleasant surprise. Come in, have a seat," he added, pushing several newspapers to the floor and pointing to the chair. Pulling his straight-backed chair closer, he said to the butler, "Bring us something to eat, Porter. Have you had breakfast yet, Cousin?"

"Yes, I did, but do you go ahead."

"Don't mind if I do. Sometimes I start working on these things and I could go for days without eating—or seeing anybody, for that matter."

"I'm glad you could see me," said Jared, noticing for the first time his cousin's rumpled evening clothes. "Out late last night?"

"What?" Casper looked down and giggled. "No, no, took mother about, but that was all. I came back and started working on this thing . . . demmed well finished it, too!" he added proudly.

He can't have had anything to do with it, reflected Jared. He doubted his cousin could be involved in anything clandestine, much less murder. The man appeared completely harmless.

"Is your mother home now?" he asked.

"Lud, I don't know. Probably, since it's sort of early, but she won't come down till late in the afternoon. That's why I don't like to sleep the morning away." Casper grinned and raised his brows toward the ceiling twice. "So devilishly pleasant at this time of day." The butler entered with a tray and set it on the table. Casper fell to eating immediately.

"Casper, do you keep any horses?"

"Yes, of course. I have a couple of hacks, and then there are mother's old plodders that pull that landau of hers. Why do you ask?"

"Just wondered. Where do you stable them?"

"Not far. It's just too demmed expensive to have a private stable. I keep them at the mews two streets over. My groom can get there and fetch them back as quick as the cat can lick its ear."

"Do you resent the fact that I inherited the title?" asked Jared forthrightly.

His cousin stopped chewing and appeared thoughtful for a moment before he leaned forward, lowering his voice, and said, "Not a bit, and it makes my mother furious!" He chuckled. "She almost turned purple when Norton told us he had located you! But me? I don't mind at all."

"You don't want the money?"

"No, not at all. My father left plenty—and, fortunately, he left it to *me,* not to Mother. She would bankrupt us in a month! But I'm careful with my money. I like prudent investments. Nothing flashy for me, thank you."

"So you could afford to keep horses here if you wanted to."

"Of course, but why should I?"

"And the title?"

"Titles mean you have to live your life according to a particular pattern," said Casper with uncanny insight. He shook his head and said dismally, "Now, to Mother, that's another matter entirely. She's"—he paused, searching for a word, his brow furrowed, before closing—"ambitious."

The door opened abruptly, and Jared's aunt stepped into the room, giving him a tight smile before turning to her son and snapping, "Why on earth would you bring the marquess into this little hole? Come into the salon!"

Said the spider to the fly, thought Jared.

Casper lost his smile and stood up, following his mother obediently. Jared followed more leisurely.

Jared remained only a few minutes more. As the front door closed, he could hear his aunt begin her lecture, her words loud and scathing.

Poor devil, thought Jared. But he felt much relieved as he walked away from the house. Casper couldn't be trying to kill him. Jared's countenance darkened, however, as he faced the fact that someone else was.

He turned at the corner, traversing two streets and easily locating the mews his cousin had described. He asked one of the grooms to point out Casper Golightly's cattle and was led down the long row to the end stalls.

Carriage horses well past their prime, two small mares—and a gelding with a flaxen mane and tail.

"Damn," he said quietly.

"Amy, I don't want to move to the town house," protested Hetty, all the while looking past her well-intended sister-in-law at the door to the salon.

Hetty, dressed in her prettiest morning gown of pale green, felt surprisingly refreshed after an evening of daydreaming instead of sleeping. Each time the door opened and Sanders stepped in to announce another visitor, her heart leaped into her mouth. This time, her insistent sister-in-law joined Harry, who had lately joined Perry Bigglesby, who had rousted the earliest visitor, Mr. Arnold, who had wanted to be congratulated and paid.

"But, Hetty, you cannot possibly plan to receive the marquess here alone!" said Amy, who could usually be counted on to be reasonable when Harry was proving difficult.

"In case you've forgotten, Amy, I spent an entire month alone with him, under the same roof!" Hetty whispered. Her brother groaned.

"Hetty, it is different now," said Harry.

"I don't see how," she replied.

"It's . . . it . . . it just is!" he said, earning an unladylike snort from his wife and a groan from his friend, whom he rounded on, saying, "Then you explain it to her, Perry!"

"I don't know that I can." The large man separated himself from the rest by going to sit at the backgammon table where he and Hetty had made their pact of friendship.

"Hetty, I have made very few demands on you in the past, but as head of our family, I am ordering you to come back and live with us under my protection. If we are going to make it through this thing intact, you must do so."

"You really must." Amy clenched Hetty's hand.

Hetty disentangled herself and rose. She walked to

her brother and kissed him on the cheek, then did the same to her sister-in-law.

"I am staying here for now. That is all there is to it. I ran away once, and only see where it led."

Both opened their mouths for another round of protests, but Hetty said firmly, "I know you are worried about my reputation, but I will survive this, no matter what the outcome may be. I suppose you could withhold my nieces and nephews from me. Other than that, you haven't a leg to stand on, I'm afraid."

"Very well. I only hope you do not regret this in the end, Hetty." Her brother took his wife's hand and led her from the room.

When the door had closed behind them, Hetty turned to her last visitor. "You're not going with them, Perry?"

"No, I'll stay here, if that's all right with you. I rather fancy a game of backgammon. Haven't had a decent match since we were at Bosworth for Christmas. Care to play?" He opened the board, readying it for a game.

Hetty joined him. "I warn you, I do not intend to stand for an interminable lecture from you."

"And you won't get one. You won last time, if I remember correctly, so I'll go first," he said, rolling the die. "Perhaps I might be able to shed a little light on why Harry and Amy were so relentless."

"Indeed? I didn't realize you had become an expert on social etiquette, Perry."

"I'm not. It's just that your situation is so very much like ours was not long ago."

He had her attention now, and all pretense of playing backgammon was forgotten.

"Remember when we were children? You were almost as close to me as you were to your brother. We were the best of friends."

"I remember. Sometimes I looked forward to seeing you more than Harry. You never treated me like a little nuisance."

"True, but when I began courting you, we could no longer be friends. Things had to change. I felt obligated to call you Lady Henrietta, and later on, when you moved here, Miss Thompson. We could no longer pretend to be just friends. Everyone knew I was courting you. If I had continued to call you Hetty, as I had when we were children, there would have been talk. When you finally sat me down and broke my heart"— he paused, clutching his chest dramatically—"then everything changed back to the way it was."

"So you could call me Hetty again." She frowned slightly.

"Quite, and we could be comfortable as friends again."

"You know, Perry, I believe I have underestimated you all these years. You have become a philosopher."

"Do you understand now why Harry and Amy think you shouldn't receive the marquess here alone?"

"Yes. Now that he and I are no longer teacher and student, we must live up to the dictates of Society," Hetty said, but there was a martial light in her eyes.

Perry chuckled. Shaking his head, he rose, leaving their game behind, and strolled toward the door.

Chuckling, he turned and said, "You have no intention of following our advice, though, do you?"

"None whatsoever, old friend."

"Good for you." He winked at her before slipping outside.

After Perry left, time weighed heavily on Hetty. She strolled through the garden, admiring the gaily colored daffodils bobbing in the slight breeze. She played her lute, singing along on several songs until Penny began to howl. She ate her solitary luncheon and answered the letter Margaret had sent from Bath. Late in the afternoon, weary and dispirited, Hetty climbed the stairs, changing into another gown for dinner.

Molly fastened the last of the tiny buttons and gave her mistress's back a rather forceful pat.

"There you go," she said.

"Thank you, Molly."

The abigail grunted a response and began to remove the pins from Hetty's hair.

"Did you wish to say something?" Hetty asked when she could no longer bear having her hair brushed with such vigor.

"Wouldn't be fitting for me to say anything," commented the maid, her lips pursed in anger.

"But I give you permission." *Anything,* Hetty thought, *would be preferable to this silent assault on my person.*

"Very well, my lady, if you insist. I think it foolish to sit around waiting for the likes of Lord Winter. I never thought he was good enough for you, and I still don't, and today just goes to show!"

"Show what?" Hetty didn't want to hear what the

forthright maid might say, but the same thoughts had been taunting her from the back of her mind all day.

Molly's eyes met Hetty's in the mirror; Hetty's began to fill with tears. The maid was instantly remorseful.

"There now, what nonsense is this, listening to a foolish old woman! Why, you know I just go on and on all day long, not making a bit of sense, that's me."

Hetty rose, her chin tremulous, but she held her head high. Impulsively, she gave the abigail a quick hug and hurried down the stairs and into the silent salon.

"I thought you'd never get here," came a deep voice from the shadows.

"Jared," breathed Hetty, hardly able to believe her eyes.

"Is that all you can say?" He stepped into the light and opened his arms. She didn't hesitate but moved into his embrace, the tears she had just overcome spilling freely as she hugged his neck, her hands clutching and stroking his broad shoulders and back.

"I thought you weren't going to come," she said, leaning away from him, then blushing as his mouth made a slow, relentless descent to hers.

His answer to her question was more than she had ever hoped for, more moving than any of the novels she had purchased from Hatchards and devoured.

When next they drew back to gaze into each other's eyes, Hetty discovered Jared was seated on the sofa and she was in his lap. She leaned her head against his shoulder and breathed deeply, savoring his cologne.

"Hetty, you know I love you." He tightened his embrace and groaned when she kissed his neck. "And you know that means I want to marry you."

She sat up straight so she could look into his eyes, searching for the telltale twinkle that meant he was only teasing her. There was no twinkle, only love and warmth.

"Aren't you going to answer me?" he asked anxiously.

Smiling, Hetty relaxed against him again. "If you are certain you wish to marry a spinster of twenty and eight, a female who is very set in her ways, who will probably forever be after you to improve your speech . . ."

He turned his head, and his mouth captured hers so all thought of speech vanished. Breathless, they paused, each intensely aware of the desire burning within, each fighting against giving in to it.

Jared groaned and moved out from under her just as the door opened and Sanders announced, "Dinner, my lord, my lady."

"In a moment," called Hetty, her voice conspicuously bright. The door closed, and they fell into a fit of the giggles.

When they could speak again, Hetty reached up to tidy her hair, and Jared tried to help, his large hands covering hers and smoothing the soft brown waves that had escaped from their pins.

"It is impossible." Hetty did her best to remain afloat as she looked into those blue eyes again.

"Go upstairs and have Molly fix it. I'll wait here," he said, his tone low and sensual.

Hetty drifted out the door and up the stairs. Jared rose, smoothing his tight breeches and wishing he had a stout drink.

"I brought you a little something, my lord, remembering how you like whiskey," said Sanders, entering with a small tray and a single glass.

"You must read minds, Sanders." Jared downed the fiery liquid in one gulp.

"It is part of my job," said the old man. "I know it is not my place, my lord, but I have been with Lady Henrietta since her aunt decided I was too old to serve and threw me out on my, er, ear."

"And you want to know what my intentions are," said Jared, grinning ruefully. "I should think at least one intention was fairly evident when you opened that door, but you mean my permanent intentions, I assume."

"Exactly, my lord." Sanders showed no amusement over the marquess's small joke.

"I'm ready." Hetty strolled into the room, her hair now smooth and tidy.

Both men, servant and lord, smiled with affection as she came forward and slipped her hand through Jared's arm.

"Yes, nice and proper again, my love." Jared glanced at the old man and smiled. "Very proper," he added, echoing Sanders's own words.

"Just so, my lord." Sanders led the way to the dining room where two places were set, Hetty's usual place at the head of the table, and one for Jared on her right side.

"Thank you, Sanders," Hetty said, smiling at the servant.

"My pleasure, my lady." The old man turned pink with pleasure.

Their meal was a simple one, the main course a harrico of mutton, one of Jared's favorites. When it was presented, he raised a brow.

After the footman had left them alone again, Jared teased, "You must have been pretty sure I would show up today."

Hetty swallowed hard and looked down at her plate, saying quietly, "I was counting on it."

"Have you always been so wise?" Jared covered her hand with his and gave it a quick squeeze before Sanders opened the door, allowing the footman to enter with the next course.

"Will there be anything else at the moment?" he asked after serving them.

"No, thank you." Jared captured Hetty's hand and refused to let go. The servants left, and he added, "They may as well grow accustomed to seeing me holding your hand. I have no intention of stopping just because they haven't enough sense to leave us alone."

"You're disgraceful," laughed Hetty.

"Only where you are concerned, my love. What's more, once we are wed, all the servants had better learn to knock and wait a moment before entering if they don't wish to be shocked by what they see."

"Jared!"

"Come to think of it . . ." He leaned over as he pulled her closer for a chaste kiss that threatened to disrupt their meal. Jared heaved a groan of frustration as he released her, sitting back and staring at the mutton with little appetite.

"You must eat," said Hetty. "You will hurt Cook's feelings. She is much more sensitive than your Mrs. Anderson."

The mention of the cook on South Audley made Hetty pause, and she suddenly realized she hadn't demanded any explanation for Angel's continued presence there.

"Jared, there is one thing—actually, it is one person—we haven't discussed."

"Who is that?" he asked, taking a bite of the stew.

Hetty's voice was frosty as she said, "I believe her name was Angel."

Jared had forgotten all about Angel, the original reason for Hetty's flight from South Audley Street and from him. The twinkle Hetty had learned meant mischief lighted his eyes, but he hid it as he echoed, "Angel?"

Hetty bristled. "You know, that female who claimed to be your wife."

"Well, that was just a misunderstanding, my love. Angel *is* someone's wife—or rather, she was. And she will be again. Soon, I believe."

"What are you talking about, Jared? I saw her not more than eight days ago when I returned to London."

"Did you speak to her?" he asked.

"Certainly not! I wouldn't have, even if I had been close enough. If I had been close enough, when she put her arms around you, I would have put a stop to it!"

Jared started laughing, unable to continue his charade. "I don't know when you saw Angel with her arms around me."

"Around your neck!" exclaimed Hetty.

The door opened and the new footman started in to clear the plates away.

"Go away!" commanded both occupants of the room, sending him scurrying.

"Hetty, I was only teasing you," Jared said, becoming vexed when she didn't soften. "Angel Grant is nothing to me, I promise you. An old friend, that's all."

"Old friends do not claim to be old wives!"

"Not in the usual course of events, perhaps, but Angel is definitely not a usual course," said Jared with a smile.

His flippant remark did nothing to alleviate Hetty's apprehension, and her eyes blazed with anger.

"Hetty, be reasonable, my love. Angel is an old friend and only an old friend." He emphasized his point by placing a gentle hand over hers.

Somewhat mollified, Hetty softened. "Then why would she say she was your wife? And what did you mean when you said she was shortly to wed someone?" she added suspiciously.

"She and Tobias Norton are betrothed. The banns have been read. They will marry in a month."

"But why is she still living with you?" asked Hetty, comforted, but not ready to capitulate.

"Living with me?" asked Jared. "She's living in the house on South Audley."

Hetty threw off his hand. "Exactly!" Angry tears sprang to her eyes, but she refused to succumb to hysterics. Instead, she glared at him, daring him to comfort her. She rose, trying to keep her dignity intact.

"Hetty, wait!" he implored, taking her by the shoulders. She wrenched herself free, but he seized one hand and turned her to face him. "I'm not living in the house on South Audley! I'm living in my town house—you remember, the one Tobias didn't want me to occupy until we had finished my transformation? Please, love, you must believe me," he begged, all thought of mischief vanished from his eyes.

"Then you were telling the truth?" she asked, afraid to hope, but too desperate to face the alternative.

"I promise, love. Cross my heart, I have never loved anyone but you."

"Oh, Jared!" she breathed, throwing her arms around his neck.

After several long kisses, interspersed with brief interruptions by the servants, Jared and Hetty agreed to forgo the remaining course and adjourn to the salon.

They spent the next few hours eradicating all the misunderstandings of the past six weeks with whispered vows and ardent embraces. Jared, ever mindful of Hetty's reputation, Sanders's warnings, and his own questionable self-control, made certain they did not get carried away.

It very nearly cost him his sanity and his physical well-being, but he managed to toe the line. His defenses weakened as Hetty began to forget herself, and he had to say good night.

"When will I see you tomorrow, my lord?" she asked, her lips in an adorable pout which almost made him take her into his arms again.

"In the morning," he whispered. "We'll have an early ride bin the park."

"Or a picnic in the country?" Her brown eyes turned the simple suggestion into a wanton invitation.

Jared laughed with delight, but he shook his head.

"Good night, my love." He kissed her fingertips as he backed away.

"Good night," Hetty said, hugging herself with happiness after he had gone.

In the front hall, Jared took Sanders to one side and asked quietly, "Is there any way to circumvent these banns?"

Sanders actually chuckled and replied, "You will need to speak to the bishop, my lord. Perhaps a note to his grace, my lady's brother, would help you secure the necessary license."

"Thank you, Sanders," said Jared. "I'll write him first thing in the morning. Good night."

"Good night, my lord. And good luck," said the butler, closing the door on their visitor, still laughing quietly.

Eleven

My true love hath my heart, and I have his,
*   By just exchange, one for the other given.*
I hold his dear, and mine he cannot miss,
*   There never was a better bargain driven.*
                                    —*Sir Philip Sidney*

Jared proceeded home that night on foot, unwilling to confine his happiness within a coach of any sort. Grinning all the way, he greeted everyone he passed, tipping his hat to a lightskirt near St. James's Street and sketching a bow to everyone from the lowliest street urchin to the finest dandy.

Whistling, he turned onto the quiet street where his town house was located. His thoughts were on Hetty and the license he hoped to obtain from the bishop. He prayed they wouldn't be forced into waiting until the banns were posted like Angel and Norton. He wasn't certain his nobility was that strong.

A footstep diverted him, and Jared moved over to allow the person to pass. Too late did he sense the danger, turning aside to receive a glancing blow. He threw one quick punch, sending the assailant flying, and then whirled around as the club of the second man came crashing down on his head. Stumbling, Jared fell to the ground. The two men grabbed him under the arms and dragged him to the waiting carriage.

"There he is, guvner. Where's our money?"

Casper Golightly handed over their wages with a trembling hand and shut the door.

He tapped the top of the carriage, saying, "Waterfront."

Scrunched up in one corner of the dirty hackney cab, Casper frowned at his cousin's still form. Hesitantly, he touch Jared's head, wincing in trepidation when his fingers came into contact with a large bump. *At least,* he thought, *he is not bleeding.*

"I hope you're happy, Mama," he muttered.

Before the carriage stopped, he could smell the river. The press gang would be waiting to receive their newest recruit. It had been a near thing, finding them and not being pressed into service himself, but fear of his mother had lent him courage, and he had met the officer of that dreaded band with great daring.

The carriage rolled to a stop, and the door opened before he had a chance to touch the handle.

"Yer got 'im?" growled the rough officer.

"Yes, he's here. Have your men take him; he's still unconscious." Casper covered his nose with a scented handkerchief when the two sailors reached inside and grabbed Jared's arms. The marquess moaned as they threw him to the ground.

"Driver, drive . . . what are you doing?" squealed

Casper as the rough sailors reached inside again and yanked him out, throwing him down beside his inanimate cousin.

"Drive on, driver," commanded the officer. The driver whipped up his tired nag and the carriage clattered away.

"You won't get away with this!" Casper scrambled away from the trio of ruffians. Rough hands picked him up by the collar, and they shook him until his eyes were rolling in his head.

"Oh, won't we? Bring them along," said the officer, giving an evil laugh. "Not a bad night's work, me lads. Get paid twice fer takin' the big fellow, and once for the little namby-pamby!"

They were dragged on board a ship and thrown into the hold. Jared landed with a loud thump and groaned again. Casper stumbled down the steps and fell into a heap, whimpering with fear. He remained where he was for a moment, listening to the rats scurrying around in the dark.

Crawling over to Jared, he began to shake him and gently slap his face. "Wake up," he whispered. "Oh, do wake up, Jared."

"Hmmph," Jared moaned. He lifted his head only to succumb to a bolt of pain.

"Jared, please wake up," begged Casper.

"Where am I?"

"On a ship."

"How . . . how did I get here? And what the devil are you doing here?" he asked, not daring to try and move again.

"Oh, Jared, I . . . I feel terrible. I . . . that is, I met

you coming home and tried to stop those scoundrels! I'm afraid they overtook me as well."

"Funny, I don't remember your being there," said Jared.

"Yes, yes, but . . ." Casper began to cry, great sobbing wails that made Jared lift his head again, ignoring the pain as he patted his cousin's shoulder.

"We'll find a way out of this," said Jared. "Chin up!"

"No-o-o . . ." cried Casper. "Save yourself, Jared. Leave me here! You don't understand!"

Jared sat up, holding his head in his hands. "What don't I understand?"

In the meager light filtering down through the opening, their eyes met, and Jared turned away.

"Save yourself," Casper reiterated. "I'll try to distract them."

Jared shook his head. "Tell me everything," he ordered.

"Well, I . . . oh, Jared, I'm so sorry!" he sobbed.

Jared gripped Casper by the shoulders and looked into his fearful eyes.

"Stop it! If we're going to escape, it will take both of us! Now, tell me what happened, and do not start bellowing again."

Casper nodded and began. "When I told Mother you planned to wed, she was very distraught."

"Go ahead," he said grimly.

"She and Sylvester kept telling me you had stolen my inheritance. I said I didn't care, and she slapped me. They sent me out of the room and talked for a while. When they called me in again, they told me they had a plan."

"Which is how we ended up here," said Jared dryly.

"Yes, except I wasn't supposed to be here!" exclaimed Casper.

"But now that you are, you want my help to escape."

"Yes. But, Jared, really, I wish none of this had happened. I don't care about the demmed title. I guess I've never been very ambitious," he admitted.

"If only you possessed the gumption to tell your mother that!" said Jared. "Anyway, it does no good to play that game. We are here, but where is that?"

"A ship, in London. Sylvester introduced me to the press gang so I could arrange your, er . . ."

"I see. Go on."

"I brought you down here after you had been knocked out. But when I turned you over to the press gang, they dragged me out of the hackney cab and took me, too!" he finished indignantly.

"Imagine," commented Jared. "What did they say when they dragged you out?"

"I told them they couldn't do that, but they ignored me. Then the one in charge said something about being paid for you twice and me once. I didn't understand that bit."

"And you said our cousin Sylvester is the one who introduced you to these gentlemen?"

"Yes, I did wonder how he came to know . . . by all that's holy, Jared! I think Sylvester double-crossed us!" exclaimed Casper.

"You mean he double-crossed you," said Jared dryly.

Casper Golightly was not a great wit, but he felt keenly the wrong he had done his American cousin. Unable to face him, he said humbly, "Jared, I am sorry."

"Never mind," said Jared. "Let's figure out how we can get out of this predicament. We can assume we have until high tide. What time do you suppose it is?" They heard a key turn in the lock and someone threw them a loaf of bread. " 'Ere's th' ale. Catch!"

Jared caught the jug and pulled the stopper, taking a long draught before handing it to Casper who drank greedily. Jared pulled it away, shaking his head.

"Drugged," he murmured, slumping down again and passing out.

Sniffling, Casper closed his eyes and fell over with a thump.

Hetty rose at eight o'clock the next morning, her spirits soaring. Molly helped her dress in her severely cut riding habit of dark green wool with the dashing hat to match.

"Eat some toast at least," coaxed the maid.

"I couldn't eat a bite, Molly. Is Ned out front with the mare?"

"Yes, my lady, he's there. Has been for the last ten minutes. He's all dressed, fine as sixpence, in his livery."

"He doesn't have to go with me," said Hetty.

"O' course he does. Now you're bein' courted by

the marquess, you must learn to keep up appearances."

"Oh, very well. I wonder where Jared is. He is not usually late. I think I'll go downstairs to wait for him."

"Not before you eat some toast, my lady," said the maid.

Hetty picked up a piece of toast and left the room, Penny trotting along at her heels. As soon as she had rounded the corner, she dropped the toast for the little dog.

Tripping lightly down the stairs, Hetty smiled brightly at Sanders and the footman before entering the salon to wait for Jared.

By ten o'clock, Hetty's impatience had turned to anger. By noon, anger had changed to concern. By four o'clock, concern progressed to anxiety, and she sent a note to Jared's staff, learning in the butler's vague response they had not seen Lord Winter since the previous afternoon.

At eight o'clock, Hetty sent another missive, this one requesting that the three runners, Taggert, Arnold, and Waller, wait on her first thing in the morning.

When Molly retrieved the tea tray with all her mistress's favorite sweets untouched, she clucked worriedly for a moment before saying, "Child, I do not wish to cause you pain, but perhaps his lordship has changed his mind."

"Never, Molly!" adjured Hetty vehemently. "He wouldn't! He couldn't!"

"But, my lady . . ."

"You don't understand!" Hetty fled from the words and her room, rushing down the steps, her face a picture of despair.

Entering the salon, she blew out all the candles and pulled a chair to the window, taking up her vigil for her betrothed.

Sanders, entering quietly some time later, said, "I have brought you a blanket, my lady, and a little something to eat."

"I couldn't." She accepted the blanket but waved the platter away. He turned to go, and Hetty asked hesitantly, "Sanders, do you think Lord Winter may have changed his mind? Molly said . . ."

"My lady, do not listen to her. Lord Winter has been detained, that is all. Some sudden business may have taken him away unexpectedly."

"But his servants said . . ."

"I daresay, their being so new to him, Lord Winter does not confide his every movement to them," said the butler. "Be patient, my lady."

"But why didn't he send word to me if he was called away?" she asked miserably, accepting a cup of hot tea from him without thinking.

"Ah, but Lord Winter is so recently betrothed, he may not have considered properly. You will make him understand, when you see him, the error of his ways," said the butler, smiling at his mistress.

Somewhat cheered, Hetty smiled. "Thank you, Sanders."

"My pleasure, my lady." The old butler kept his head erect until he had closed the door on his melancholy mistress.

He crooked a finger at the footman. "Follow me," he commanded, leading the way to Hetty's small study. Taking pen and paper, Sanders scribbled a hasty note,

sanded it, and placed it in an envelope. Taking a heavy
seal and wax from the drawer, he melted the wax and
pressed the heavy seal of the Duke of Bosworth into
it before handing it to the footman.

"Take this to Bow Street."

"But, Mr. Sanders, I already went to Bow Street
once today."

"Just do as you are told, Robbie. This note will set
in motion certain inquiries immediately. Though I
wouldn't wish to tell the mistress, I fear we cannot
wait until morning to begin the search for Lord Winter."

"But, Mr. Sanders," said the younger man, "do you
not think it likely Lord Winter has had second
thoughts?"

"It is not for you to judge your betters," said Sanders, his rebuke softened by weariness and doubt.
"However, our mistress is often too kind, and we must
do what we can to help her."

"Anything, Mr. Sanders!" said the footman, pocketing the envelope and hurrying away.

Jared wished it wasn't necessary, but he knew he
had to open his eyes. He had been lying still for some-
time since regaining consciousness, trying to remember how he came to be in such a dark, dank,
foul-smelling place. The thought he was once again
in prison struck panic in his breast, but he recognized
the gentle swaying of a ship and realized such was
not the case.

Feeling the tender bump on his head, he recalled

the altercation with the ruffians in the street. This memory led him to open his eyes and search the darkened hold for his cousin. He found him moments later, still dead to the world.

"Casper," he whispered, his throat dry and scratchy. "Wake up, old man, wake up." Feeling for the jug of ale, Jared soaked his handkerchief with the cold liquid and bathed his cousin's face.

"What?" groaned Casper, sitting up suddenly. "What happened?"

"We were drugged."

"What time is it?" asked Casper, his eyes searching the gloom for the stairs leading to the exit.

"I don't know. It's too dark to see."

"Are we moving?" asked Casper.

"I don't think so. I think we're still moored."

"How long do you suppose we have been down here?"

Jared felt for the steps and climbed up to the opening. It was covered by a heavy grate. He pushed on it, but couldn't budge it. Through a small hole, he could see the moon.

"Moon rise," he muttered. "Looks as if we slept through the day."

"Gadzooks, but I'm thirsty."

"Don't drink the ale," warned Jared, pushing against the grate again.

"I'm not that stupid," said his cousin. "Why the devil do you keep pushing on that? You know it's locked."

"Not locked, just fastened. If I can . . . oomph!" he grunted, pressing his shoulders upward with all his might. Sliding his fingers through the small fissure, he tried to dislodge the rod inserted through the hinge.

"Did you . . ."

"Ow!" Jared forced himself to lift the grate once more to free his smashed fingers. "Argh!" he groaned, sliding down the steps, nursing his hand.

"Are they broken?" Casper asked anxiously, grabbing Jared's hand and moving each finger.

"Do you mind?" Jared snatched his hand back. "I'll be all right. They're not broken!"

Casper leaned against the steps and declared gloomily, "It's no use. We may as well get used to it. We can't escape."

"Don't lose your nerve now, Casper. We have to stick together."

"Of course, Jared, but it's hopeless."

"Devil a bit. Did I tell you what I was facing when Norton found me? No? Well, it was ten times worse than this!" said Jared stoutly. "The hangman was measuring me for a noose, and look at me now!"

In the moonlight, he could just make out his cousin's ironic expression.

"Okay, not now, but before we ended up here," Jared said. "We have to have a plan, that's all."

"And what might that be? Starting a fire so they'll have to let us out? We'll have suffocated or roasted by then," said Casper.

"Not a bad idea, but I think we can come up with a better plan. I've seen you at Jackson's Boxing Salon, Casper. You're not half bad. Between us, we might be able to overpower the guards when they bring us food."

"If they do," Casper muttered. At Jared's disgusted curse, he returned, "All right, all right. It's worth a try. Anything to get out of here." He lowered his voice, saying, "I don't think we are alone."

"Not alone?" asked Jared. "Ah, you mean the rats. Yes, I had noticed. Keep alert. They won't bother you."

Arnold was chosen to report to Lady Hetty the next morning. The three Bow Street runners had drawn straws, and he had lost. Weeping females, they all agreed, were the most difficult part of their job—any job!

But Hetty was not weeping when Arnold entered the salon of the house on Cavendish Square. She was dressed for riding and was pacing the room.

"I need your help again, Mr. Arnold," she said, pausing to address him.

"Yes, my lady, I know," said the puzzled runner.

"What do you mean, you know?" she asked.

Sanders cleared his throat and said, "Pardon me, my lady, but I took the liberty last night of sending a missive to Mr. Arnold, requiring him to begin his search immediately. I beg your pardon," he added humbly.

"No need, Sanders. You were right to do so." Hetty turned back to the runner. "And have you discovered Lord Winter's whereabouts, Mr. Arnold?"

He grimaced, shifting from one foot to the other on the thick Aubusson carpet. "I'm afraid we can't find any trace of his lordship, my lady. The three of us,

Taggert, Waller, and me, we've been up all night, but
it's like he vanished without a trace."

"Then you must continue to search for him!" said
Hetty, her dismay showing plainly on her face.

The runner began to back away, saying, "Yes, my
lady. Right away, my lady." Almost running, he made
good his escape before the tears began to flow.

With faltering tread, Hetty reached the sofa and sat
down heavily. Sanders disappeared, returning minutes
later with a glass of dark liquid.

"Drink this, my lady. It will steady your nerves."

She obeyed, so distracted she didn't even sputter
when the fiery liquid burned its way down her throat.

"Shall I send for her grace?" he asked.

"No, not yet. Tell Ned to saddle my mare, Sanders.
I'm going for a ride."

Clearly agitated, Sanders hesitated. Smiling up at
him, Hetty said, "Don't worry, Sanders. I promise to
take the groom with me, and I will only ride in the
park. I'm not going to look for Lord Winter on my
own. What would I do if I found him and he didn't
wish to be found? Especially by me!" She gave a self-
deprecating laugh, adding, "Go ahead. I promise I'll
be sensible."

Their plans made, Jared and Casper rested throughout the morning, each doing his best to ignore his
gnawing hunger and raging thirst.

Time crawled until finally they heard footsteps and
the sound of the latch being shifted. Casper threw himself facedown at the foot of the stairs while Jared,

climbing on the underside of the steps, waited in silence for their captors to move the grate. With much
grunting and groaning, the grate fell away from the
opening and sunlight shone down, alleviating the terrible blackness of their prison. Jared blinked, letting
his eyes adjust to the light. The sailor peered into the
black hold, the single spot of light showing only one
man, silent and still.

"Wot's th' matter?" called someone from behind the
sailor.

"Nothin'. That cove as what hired us 'pears dead,"
he replied dispassionately.

"Where's th' other "un?"

"Don' know." He placed his booted foot on the top
step.

Jared waited. The man lowered a lantern, descending one more rung and bending over as he peered into
the recesses of the floating dungeon. In a smooth,
swift movement, Jared grabbed the man's leg and
flung him down the steps where Casper, coming to
life, began to beat him about the head.

Jared swung around to the top of the steps just as
the other rogue began to shift the grate over the opening. Thrusting upward with all his might, Jared threw
the man backwards onto the deck. Not pausing to see
if anyone else was about to join the fray, Jared dove
for his captor, pummeling him in the face before a
blow sent him reeling. Circling warily, Jared heard the
struggle taking place below. He glanced toward the
opening behind him.

The sailor took advantage of his distraction and
charged, head down. Jared's fists met the man's thick

neck as he stepped out of the way, sending the sailor stumbling forward. He screamed as he fell into the dark hole.

"Casper!" called Jared.

His cousin appeared in the opening, ragged and bleeding. Jared stretched out his hand and pulled him out as the second sailor tried to catch hold. Casper gave the man a mighty kick, and he fell with a thud. Together, the cousins replaced the grate before turning and congratulating each other.

They traversed the deck warily, prepared to meet another challenger, but none appeared, and they crossed the gangplank to the bank.

"You look like the very devil, Jared." Casper winced when he smiled and stretched his broken lip.

"Some of these bruises I earned before reaching the ship," Jared said dryly.

Casper Golightly stopped in his tracks, grimacing with embarrassment. "I'm sorry, coz. I shouldn't have let my mother talk me into having you pressed into the navy."

"Casper, I don't think that was an ordinary press gang. I think they meant to kill us."

Casper appeared much struck by this. At length, he snapped his fingers, saying, "Sylvester! He's the one who put me onto those three!"

"I thought as much," said Jared. "With both of us out of the way, he would have inherited."

"But he couldn't have if there was no proof we were dead."

"After another day or two, we might well have been. It was a perfect plan. We're taken by the press gang, we get killed. No one knows where we are until our bodies wash up in the Thames and Sylvester becomes the Marquess Winter."

"The bloody butcher," murmured Casper as they continued on their way. Then he paused again. "You don't suppose my mother knew all that?"

Privately, Jared thought his cold-blooded aunt capable of much more, but he shook his head and said, "No, she just wanted you to inherit." They were away from the wharves by now and tried to hire a hackney to take them up, but their bloody appearances made the drivers refuse.

"Never mind, Casper. It's not too far," Jared said as they continued on foot. Jared paused to catch his breath and asked, "By the way, do you often ride that gelding with the flaxen mane and tail?"

"What gelding? Oh, you mean Sylvester's horse. No, I prefer my gentle old mare."

Slapping his cousin on the back, Jared said, "Let's go home, Casper. If the cook doesn't have dinner waiting on us, we'll eat it raw!"

"Please, my lady, Mr. Sanders made me promise to bring you straight home from the park," said the miserable Ned. Sanders had sent him to accompany her in place of the regular groom, thinking the older man would have more influence on his mistress.

"Ned, you need not go with me. I can manage quite well on my own," said Hetty, head held high as she rode through the busy streets.

It was close to five o'clock, and the roads leading

to Hyde Park were filled with the fashionables making their way to Rotten Row. Ned ducked his head, continuing doggedly on in silent resignation.

Hetty ignored the curious glances she received as well as the appreciative, if inappropriate, greetings from strange gentlemen. Finally, she reached her destination and dismounted without waiting for assistance before throwing the reins to Ned.

"Walk the horses," she commanded, climbing the steps of Jared's impressive town house.

Ned waited until she had been admitted before leading the horses a short distance down the street.

"I wish to see Lord Winter," said Hetty, her voice a study in aristocratic hauteur.

Martin was in a quandary. Jared's new butler noticed the quiet elegance of her riding habit and acknowledged she was quality, despite the irregularity of her visit to a bachelor abode, but what to do with her?

"I beg your indulgence, madam . . ."

"Lady Henrietta," she corrected, her nose elevating another notch. The butler began to perspire and apologized profusely.

"Indeed, my lady, Lord Winter is not at home."

Now it was Hetty's turn to study the servant, her scrutiny causing him physical discomfort.

"Gibbons," she said simply. "I will speak to Gibbons."

"His lordship's valet?" asked the incredulous butler.

"Indeed." She speared him with those eyes again.

"Very well, my lady. If you would be so good as to step into"—he swallowed convulsively; he had been about to lead her to the tiny alcove reserved for unimportant, uninvited visitors—"the salon," he finished, breathing a sigh of relief.

In the normal course of events, Hetty would have been pleased by the simple furnishings in the room, but they held little interest for her in her present state of mind. She was still standing when the door opened minutes later, and the distracted valet rushed into the room.

"My lady!" he intoned, forgetting to bow as he showed her to the sofa, all the while wringing his hands. "Have you any word of Lord Winter?"

Hetty expelled her pent-up breath. The valet's reaction to her visit surprised her, she realized. She had been half-expecting to discover Jared was merely avoiding her. Now she had to face the truth. He was missing, very likely hurt, perhaps . . . no, she couldn't face that possibility.

"When did you last see him?" she asked quietly.

The valet, forgetting himself, dropped down by her side and covered his face with his hands, saying in muffled tones, "I thought . . . I hoped he was with you, my lady."

Hetty patted his shoulder and shook her head.

"What are we to do?" he asked.

"I have already notified the authorities, Gibbons. But tell me, when was the last time you saw his lordship?"

"It was two days ago. He had on his gray coat and a blue waistcoat. He came to my room and told me he wanted to look his best for you," he ended with a sniffle.

"And he did," she said, smiling through a cloud of

unshed tears. Puzzled, Hetty added, "But why did he come to your room?"

"I was in bed after my ordeal," explained the valet, his eyes widening when he read the confusion in her eyes. "You didn't know? Someone shot me!"

Hetty felt the room begin to spin. "Why would anyone shoot you, Gibbons?" she asked, giving control to her more reasonable side.

"They thought it was his lordship, and it wasn't the first time!"

"But why? Why would . . . money! Of course! It must have been that Casper Golightly."

"I believe that is what they are investigating, my lady."

Hetty was trembling now, and the valet asked anxiously, "Is there anything I can do?" Rising, he squared his shoulders with newfound dignity.

"We are doing everythi—"

"Hetty!" The laughing marquess threw open the door to the salon and crossed it in three strides, taking her into his arms and planting a kiss on her open lips.

"Jared! Jared!" she exclaimed, pushing back in his embrace and taking his bruised face in her hands. "Thank God!" she whispered before returning his kiss and throwing her arms around his neck.

"Lord Winter!" exclaimed the valet.

"Gibbons!" the butler said sternly from the doorway.

The valet glanced at his master and Lady Henrietta once more, heaved a relieved sigh, and left the room. Casper, who had stepped into the salon on the heels of his cousin, watched for a moment, then smiled and shut the door.

"Do you think you could manage a bath and a change of clothes for me, Gibbons? I would probably give my mother apoplexy if I turn up looking like this."

"Certainly, Mr. Golightly," said Gibbons, quickly forgetting he had lately accused the marquess's cousin of attempted murder.

Casper took a step toward the stairs and hesitated, a thoughtful mien in place of his usually vapid countenance.

"On second thought, Gibbons, I think I'll go straight home. I have a thing or two to tell my mother, and I find it can't wait another minute. Tell my cousin I will wait on him here at eight o'clock tomorrow morning."

"Very good, Mr. Golightly," said Martin, once more prim and proper.

Inside the salon, Jared reluctantly pulled himself away from Hetty. "I am filthy, my love. I'm ruining your pretty gown."

"I don't care if you do," she said, wrapping her arms around him and squeezing him tightly. "I am never going to let you out of my sight again!"

"This could get interesting." Jared took her hand in his and kissed each fingertip, letting the tip of his tongue tease each finger in turn. Hetty shivered, sidling closer to him.

"I need a bath," he said.

"Yes, you do," she whispered.

"Are you still not going to let me out of your sight?" He gave her a scandalous leer.

"Let me amend that, my lord. I will not let you leave this house without me, but you may go and have your bath while I wait here."

Giving her lips a light kiss, Jared rose and walked to the door. "Can you stand to be parted from me for so long?" he quipped.

"Now you are being conceited," she admonished, laughing out loud when the door closed behind him. Rising, Hetty waltzed around the salon, humming the same tune, though not as expertly, Jared had when they danced on their picnic.

A moment later, she looked impatiently at the clock over the mantle and frowned. Just how long did it take a man to bathe?

Twelve

Thou art my life, my love, my heart,
The very eyes of me;
And hast command of every part,
To live and die for thee.

—Robert Herrick

Taggert bowed his head as he admitted defeat. The other two runners did the same. "We've got no excuse, milord. We just can't find the culprit. We think he's most likely fled the country," finished Taggert, finally daring to look into the marquess's cold eyes.

"I want proof," Jared said. "If he has gone, someone has to have seen him. He had to pay his way, something I doubt he is capable of doing, or he has to work his passage out. You should be able to trace that."

"We've tried, milord," said Taggert. "We went as far as Brighton, but no luck."

"Taggert, are you married?"

"Yes, milord."

"Children?"

"Five."

"What would you do in my place, knowing your wife and children were in danger? I'm getting married on Saturday morning. By marrying me, my future wife is in danger. I want to do everything I can to protect her. You gentlemen are that everything. I'm counting on you."

Taggert stood a little straighter as he faced Jared and said, "Thank you, milord. Speaking for myself, Waller, and Arnold, here, we'll see to it you and your new wife are completely safe."

Jared shook each man's hand and thanked them. When the runners had gone, he sat back and closed his eyes. The movement still hurt a little, but the swelling was almost gone, and he hoped the discoloration would be gone by Saturday.

"Her grace, the Duchess of Bosworth to see you, my lord," said Jared's proper butler. "Lady Hetty also," added Martin, almost choking on the shortened name.

Hetty crossed the floor and put her arms around Jared's neck, giving him a kiss and a hug.

"Enough of that!" said Amy, laughing at them. Jared took Hetty's hand and led her to the sofa, seating Amy in the chair beside it.

"What brings you so early, my dear?" he asked, keeping her hand in his and rubbing his thumb along the palm.

After a moment, Amy prodded her sister-in-law. "Hetty! Do pay attention!"

"What?" she said, causing Jared to chuckle and withdraw his hand from hers.

"You would not make a very good teacher these days, my sweet," he laughed. "Now, what can I do for you?"

"Oh, I wanted to know if you liked lobster. We thought to have that for the fish course at the wedding breakfast, but I wasn't certain you cared for it."

"A matter of some importance, this visit," said Amy.

"Indeed it is. As a matter of fact, I love lobster. That's an excellent choice. By the way, Hetty, I needed to ask you something." Jared's blue eyes twinkled dangerously.

"What is that?" she asked, keeping her own eyes wide and innocent and refraining from smiling at him.

"The gardener wanted to know where to place the daffodils in our garden here. I told him you would have to be consulted."

"Oh, why don't we take a look now?" answered Hetty, rising and starting for the door.

"I'll come along, too," Amy said.

"No!" said the couple as one.

Gurgling with laughter, Amy said, "You have ten minutes in the garden alone. After that, I will come in and pull you out by your hair if I have to, Lady Henrietta."

Jared pulled Hetty out the door and along the garden path until they were secluded from prying eyes.

Several kisses later, as Hetty rested her head on his chest, Jared breathed, "What day is this?"

"Thursday," whispered Hetty.

"I don't think I'll make it until Saturday," declared Jared, diving for another taste of her lips.

"Hetty! We must be going!" called Amy, true to her word.

Jared groaned, kissed Hetty one last, lingering time, and pushed her toward her sister-in-law. Waving at them, he called, "I'm just going to stay out here. I'll see you at dinner tonight," he added, blowing a kiss to Hetty. She smiled, and Amy laughingly returned it.

Hetty's wedding day dawned bright and clear. She rose early, before Molly came to wake her. She was, in truth, too excited to sleep. The past week had been hectic for everyone once she and Jared had agreed on the time and date for the service. Harry had introduced Jared to the bishop and arranged for the special license.

Amy, who had three sisters, enlisted the aid of every one of them as she issued invitations for the wedding breakfast to their closest friends, some one hundred fifty people. The children were outfitted in matching gowns and suits and instructed on how they should dispense the white rose petals as their father escorted their aunt down the aisle, and Amy's wedding gown was hastily altered and lengthened to fit Hetty's long frame and noble bustline.

Hetty had been persuaded to remove to her brother's town house until after the ceremony, another factor which contributed to her lack of sleep for the past few nights as she struggled to adjust to the bustle of a large household.

Saturday morning finally arrived, and Hetty waited impatiently for the clock to chime half past nine so they could begin the short journey to the church.

Molly entered with a heart-shaped note and handed it to Hetty. Standing back to admire the gown, she covered her face with her apron and sobbed.

Hetty comforted her, and she sniffed, "I'm so happy for you, my lady."

"Thank you, Molly. I am very happy, too." She opened the note. In childish letter, it read:

> *I reckon we're finally gittin' hitched, Miss Thompson. See yer at ten o'clock.*
>
> *Yer lovin' student,*
> *Jared*

She hugged it to her bosom and chortled with happiness.

"I know one thing," she said to the smiling abigail, "I will never be bored!" She gave Molly a hug and danced toward the door.

Harry was waiting on the other side, looking thoughtful. With a jerk of his head, he sent the maid away. Studying his sister, he smiled.

"So you really are going through with it."

Hetty nodded. "I love him, Harry."

"I know you do. At least this time you don't have to wonder if he is wedding you for your connections or fortune."

"Even if Jared were poor, I wouldn't have any qualms, Harry. I am that certain. Not even Papa could convince me Jared doesn't love me for myself."

Harry gave his twin a hug and tucked her hand into the crook of his arm.

"That's all I wanted to know," he said. "Shall we go?"

"Oh, yes!" she declared happily.

"Quit fidgeting," whispered Casper as he and Jared awaited the bridal party at the front of the church. "Everyone's going to think you're nervous about getting married."

"I am," whispered Jared. "Only a fool wouldn't be nervous about standing up in front of all these people and pledging his life to one woman."

"You're not going to back out!" hissed his cousin, truly alarmed.

The music began, and Hetty's nieces and nephews started slowly down the aisle. Behind them came their mother, whispering words of encouragement, then Harry appeared with Hetty on his arm. He was two inches shorter than she, but they were resplendent in their wedding finery.

Jared's eyes met Hetty's, and he relaxed.

"Well, are you?"

"Am I what?"

"Backing out."

"Not in a million years," Jared said, accepting Hetty's hand from Harry and turning to face the bishop.

"The wedding breakfast will go on for hours, Hetty, but there is no reason for you and Jared to remain that long." Amy stood back to inspect her sister-in-law's new yellow carriage dress and bonnet. "Perfect!" She looked to Molly for confirmation.

"Absolutely, your grace," said the abigail with pride.

There was a knock on the door, and Hetty gazed with shining eyes as Jared stepped into the room.

"Handsome as ever," she said, smiling for him alone.

He crossed to her side and lifted her hand to his lips. "Beautiful as ever," he said.

Molly sniffed and gave her mistress a final hug. Amy also hugged Hetty, and then hugged Jared for good measure.

"Take care of her," she admonished.

"I plan to."

Jared led Hetty from the room and down the stairs, where the throng of well-wishers swelled in number as people on the street joined the celebration, calling out their congratulations and advice to the newlyweds.

As Jared handed Hetty into the carriage, she looked closely at the grooms hanging onto the back straps. When they were finally away, Jared took Hetty into his arms and kissed her, pulling her onto his lap so he could hold her close.

"I wish you would tell me where we were going," she said, resting her head on his shoulder after several more kisses.

"Very well, I will. We are driving to Dover, where we will spend the night. Tomorrow, we sail for France."

"We're going to Paris?" asked Hetty. "How wonderful!"

"Thank you. I thought you needed a chance to practice your French," he teased.

"And the two runners, are they going all the way to Paris with us?"

Jared frowned. "You weren't supposed to notice Taggert and Waller."

"Waller, too. I only saw Arnold and Taggert." Hetty snuggled closer and shivered. "So you think Sylvester still wants to kill you."

"No, not at all. Taggert and his men are just with us until we set sail, my love. I didn't want anything to happen. It is merely a precaution. I expect my cousin is halfway across the world by now."

"I pray you are right, Jared."

"What time is it?" whispered Hetty, raising up on one elbow to see Jared's face in the firelight.

"It's late, my love. Time for all good girls to be asleep."

Hetty ran her hand down his chest, letting her fingers twirl the dark hair surrounding his navel. Jared turned, trapping her hand between them.

"I warned you, Marchioness Winter," he murmured quietly. "Now you're in for it."

Hetty giggled as his kisses began, light and teasing. Then he pulled her on top of him. Her laughter ceased, replaced by a moan of pleasure.

* * *

Morning brought the packet that would carry them to France. Taggert and his associates helped load the luggage on board before going ashore, waiting for the ship to sail. Gibbons and Molly, who had followed in a separate carriage with the boxes, set about stowing the luggage and making the cabin tidy for their mistress and master.

Jared and Hetty remained at the far rail, watching the expanse of water, hoping for a glimpse of the other coast, since the day was fair. The sailors slipped the moorings, and the boat moved away from the shore. Returning to the dockside rail, Hetty and Jared waved to the three runners.

Jared, putting his arm around his wife, asked, "Do you want to stay topside or go below?"

"I think I will go below for now, Jared." Hetty yawned daintily. "I find I am absolutely exhausted."

"Too exhausted?" he whispered in her ear.

Hetty laughed and shrugged her shoulders. Jared groaned. He didn't know he could want a woman as much as he wanted Hetty . . . or as often, came the lascivious thought.

Still, he would give her a few minutes by herself. She probably needed to take care of other needs. He turned back to the rail, watching Taggert shrink smaller and smaller.

The runner waved, and Jared responded in kind. Curious, he thought, watching as a small boat with two men in it set out in pursuit of the large packet.

"What the deuce?" he muttered, frowning as the runner on shore began to jump up and down, waving his arms like a madman.

"Jared!" Hetty screamed.

Jared whirled around.

"Sylvester, let go of her," Jared said. "It's me you want."

"No, no! It's both of you now!"

Sylvester's eyes were red and bloodshot, as if he hadn't slept in the past week. And he had Hetty.

"Jared," cried Hetty again.

"Be calm." He inched closer.

"Stay where you are!" Sylvester shouted. They were attracting a crowd now, and several sailors started forward. "Tell them to get away, or I'll slit her throat!" he warned. Sunlight flashed on the blade of his knife.

"Get away! I'll handle this," commanded Jared. "Let her go, cousin. Get rid of me, and then you can be the new marquess," he lied.

Sylvester let loose a deranged laugh. "No, no, I can't do that now. Not after last night." Hetty gasped as he tightened his grip around her neck. "She's probably with child already. How many times was it? I grew tired of counting," he said.

Jared lost his temper then and lunged. Sylvester dragged Hetty away and placed the knife at her throat again. Jared backed away.

Tears sprang to Hetty's eyes and her stomach began to roll. He had been at the inn, someplace close by. Nausea threatened to overwhelm her. Sylvester's hand brushed her breast as he dragged her closer to the rail. Breakfast, which had seemed so appetizing before sailing, rose in her throat and Hetty gagged, then retched horribly.

Sylvester threw her away from him in disgust, and Jared snatched his opportunity, closing in for the kill, flying at his cousin and sending him sprawling. They circled, Sylvester waving his knife inexpertly. Jared feinted to the right as his cousin charged.

A shot rang out. On the railing, Sylvester's body stiffened. His arms outstretched, he resembled a child's teeter-totter. In slow motion, he tilted over the rail and fell into the cold water.

Jared pulled Hetty into his arms, covering her ears from Sylvester's maniacal screams until the water silenced them. They watched as Arnold put aside his pistol and helped retrieve the body, pulling it into the skiff. He saluted Jared and rowed back to shore.

Jared took Hetty below, where Molly cleaned her up and tucked her into the bed. It took all his self-control to remain topside, allowing the laudanum the ship's cook prescribed time to work. After an hour, he could stand it no longer and entered their tiny cabin.

"Jared?" she whispered, opening her eyes and searching for him. "Is it really over?"

"Yes, it's over. Rest now," he advised, stroking her soft brown hair.

"I refused to take the laudanum," she said, smiling at him.

"You don't look like you refused," chuckled Jared. "You look like you are about to fall asleep."

"That ish an act, my dear hushband," Hetty said. She turned on her side and scrunched up against the wall, holding out her arms. "Lie down with me," she whispered, her lips pouting and her eyes closed.

Jared grinned and joined her, half hanging off the tiny bunk. But she snuggled against him, sighing contentedly.

"I love you, Jared Winter," she murmured.

"And I love you, Miss Thompson," he replied, kissing the top of her head as she finally found rest in his arms.

Put a Little Romance in Your Life With
Fern Michaels